Waking Dead

Waking Dead

a novel

Jay Glendell

WAKING DEAD
A NOVEL

iUniverse books may be ordered through booksellers or by contacting:

iUniverse
1663 Liberty Drive
Bloomington, IN 47403
www.iuniverse.com
1-800-Authors (1-800-288-4677)

ISBN: 978-1-5320-5376-4 (sc)
ISBN: 978-1-5320-5377-1 (e)

Library of Congress Control Number: 2018908791

Print information available on the last page.

iUniverse rev. date: 09/18/2018

Chapter One

⟤━◆━⟤

I can't catch my breath; a black wall is crushing my chest. No air is getting into my lungs, and the pressure is unbearable. Suffocating and paralyzed, I will stop breathing! I'm dying he thought, terrified of what was next. The alarm went off; it's five AM, the worst time of the day for Paul Peres. Drenched in a cold sweat, he dreaded the early hour. It was the time of the day when men seldom survived the widow maker, a blockage of the main artery of the heart muscle that kills suddenly in the early morning hours while asleep in bed. The nightmare had been repeating more frequently, leaving him in a dream-like state, semi-conscious but paralyzed and speechless. Each time, he'd remain horrified by the thought that he was dead and lingered in a conscious state. Some of his patients brought back from the brink of death told him that they had died but were fully aware of what was happening around them and couldn't communicate or react. Rationally, Paul knew that what he had endured was not a near death experience but only night terrors with sleep paralysis. However, he couldn't shake the feeling that he had been dying and waking dead.

He hurried to the hospital earlier than usual to review the charts of patients scheduled to be seen in the afternoon medical clinic. As the director of the outpatient department, his job was to supervise the interns and residents in the clinic. Paul, an internist and full-time employee of North County Hospital had been subpoenaed by his wife's attorney to appear in court that afternoon. His wife sought sole custody of the children and had charged him with child neglect and abandonment. His life was in a tailspin with the uncertain future of his employment at the hospital and the stress of the divorce. Appearing in court at that time conflicted with the clinic and he decided to leave detailed instructions on each patient's chart, so the interns and residents could function without him. A covering doctor had been assigned to take his place that afternoon, but Paul was not confident he could depend on him. A mistake would get him fired.

He arrived at the hospital and entered the cafeteria for a cup of coffee. It was usually a busy place but appeared deserted at that hour, except for someone slumped over a table, at the other end of the room. He walked over to the table and realized it was Raj, a pathologist, and friend who worked there. Raj cradling the dining room table with his hair rumpled up and face covered with both hands, didn't see him. Paul hearing his muted sobs tapped his shoulder and asked what was wrong. He had never seen him in a disheveled state since his friend always appeared impeccably dressed, dapper and debonair. Raj's voice cracked with barely audible sound, while he told Paul about his former wife, Elaine, who was murdered the previous evening. The police had called him early that morning to identify the body that was found in her apartment. Shocked, Paul sat next to him with his arm around his shoulders steadying him as Raj cried, and told him the harrowing details of Elaine's murder, describing it with startling precision.

The body was found dismembered with her arms and legs scattered throughout the apartment. On the dining room wall were pinned her amputated breasts staring at him as he entered the room. They seemed surgically removed as in a double mastectomy. Her stomach and intestines floated in a fish tank filled with blood red water surrounded by dead fish. Raj said the blood covered walls filled the apartment with the stench of death. Continuously shaking his head from side to side while sobbing he cried that it was the work of a human monster. He purposely didn't mention the mutilation of the genitalia and rectum, to preserve her dignity and to spare disturbing his friend further. Paul knew Elaine and was visibly shaken as he imagined the entire bloody scene. Raj insisted a surgeon or pathologist had performed the mutilation with such meticulous technique that only a doctor trained in surgical anatomy could have been responsible. He told Paul that the police believed the crime was drug-related.

Paul had difficulty regaining his composure and with a look of disbelief shouted, "Drugs!"

The word reverberated off the cold tile cafeteria walls as though there was a chorus echoing it. The cops claimed that Raj's former wife was stealing ketamine from the research lab and selling it to drug dealers. The ketamine used in the research lab to sedate animals was sold on the street as "Special K," a popular dance club drug. Vials of ketamine along with needles and syringes were found in her apartment. Raj told the police it had to be a set up to hide the real reason for her murder. He said that Elaine hated recreational drugs and never used them when she was married to him. He was unsure why anyone would do such a terrible thing and could not think of anyone who wanted her dead. Everyone admired her good looks, intelligence, and carefree spirit and she had no known enemies on the staff. She was a flirt, and Paul thought possibly a jealous wife or girlfriend murdered her, but it seemed macabre and too ordered to be the result of jealous rage.

Iraj Mussomi (called Raj by his friends and colleagues), had immigrated to the USA after finishing medical training in Italy. Born in Iran, he decided not to return to his family's homeland after the Ayatollah and his followers came to power. Raj's family belonged to an opposing political faction in Iran, so he sought asylum in the USA. A big handsome man with a dark complexion, piercing brown eyes and a large stock of white hair, he was usually mistaken for someone of Latin or Mediterranean origin. His appearance was an asset in a Westchester community of New York with a significant portion of the population from families' originating or the descendants of immigrants from Italy and Central and South America. Paul was born in the States, and his parents were from Puerto Rico. Raj's foreign accent and fluency in the Italian language acquired during his years living in Italy gave rise to many patients identifying him as an Italian. Paul' s heritage was more challenging to discern, and some thought he was Italian, and others considered him Hispanic. Raj could fool many with his comical Italian posturing and gestures and was the quintessential Italophile whose love of everything Italian included reading the Italian newspapers every day. His spontaneity performing Italian operatic arias with hysterical gestures amused the nurses of Italian descent who enjoyed his ability to brighten their day.

Paul asked if there was anything he could do to help him. Raj nodded no and said he would stay in the cafeteria waiting for the final report of the autopsy that was still underway. Although divorced from Elaine for several years, he continued to love her and be her confidant. Paul disturbed by her murder, and his friend's anguish couldn't get the incident out of his mind. He remembered how Raj had helped him when he first joined the hospital staff. They often had lunch together in the same cafeteria talking about professional and personal matters. They were from differing ethnic backgrounds than most of the physicians on the staff which created a special bond. Paul was an only child, and Raj was like an older brother that he had never had. He recalled that when Elaine and Raj were married, she was cheating on him and sexually involved with other men. Raj was heartsick when learning of it, however, the inner turmoil didn't paralyze his ability to function. He was ten to fifteen years older than Elaine and realized her free spirit and a monogamous marriage were not compatible.

Paul finally walked into the medical clinic to review patient charts gathered for the afternoon clinic. No one else was in the clinic at that hour, and the atmosphere was chilling and gloomier than usual. His sorrow was intensified by the nauseating antiseptic smell and faded inhospitable green walls that deepened his depressed state of mind. Vintage wooden examining tables covered with frayed mats and shimmering mercury columns of the blood pressure units hanging on the walls interrupted the monotony of the clinic's drab appearance. One exception to the decaying presence that surrounded him was a brand-new computer set upright on a tattered grey metal desk. He reflected on how a modern machine in the vintage setting surrounding him seemed, somehow out of place, like him. Put there to modernize medical records, the new technology failed to transform the atmosphere of a hospital that no longer succeeded in providing health services in a changing world.

While attempting to focus on patients' charts, his mind wandered and recalled his feelings about his friend and Elaine. Everyone had warned Raj of her history of affairs with other men, but he was dazzled by her beauty and intelligence and unable to see what others saw of a relationship that would fail. Before they were married, she worked in the same hospital unit as Raj, but regulations forbade married couples from working together in the same department. She applied for a position in the surgical research laboratory evaluating drugs used in the treatment of patients receiving organ transplants. Her area of expertise was pharmacology and the medicines used to treat patients receiving organ transplants were often problematic due to drug interactions that interfered with the function of the transplanted organ. The job was a natural for her and she was immediately hired.

Recalling his friendship with Elaine and Raj cut into the time to complete his morning duties and hospital rounds with the interns and residents had to be reduced to discussing each patient's progress in the hallway rather than at the patient's bedside. Before leaving the hospital, he interrupted the chief resident's morning report with the director of medicine to remind her to keep an eye on the afternoon clinic. The director of medicine, Doctor Albert Stark, scowled at Paul chewing him out for leaving early and not being present to supervise the clinic. Paul reminded Stark that he was given no option for choosing the day or time for the court hearing and sarcastically thanked him for his cooperation as he walked away to finish rounds and leave the hospital. On leaving the hospital, he drove to the courthouse.

Private insurance funds and donations supported North County Hospital, a small nonprofit hospital with both teaching and research programs that had been established in prior years. The cost of maintaining the programs had drastically risen, and with Medicare and Medicaid cutbacks the hospital lost money each year. The hospital was at the point of bankruptcy and to continue to operate had to eliminate those programs or close its doors. The only hope for its survival was a bailout from a medical school or corporative healthcare provider. A prestigious medical school had approached the hospital administration for a possible affiliation, and the public relations department presented the possible association to the local newspapers as a significant step toward providing improved medical care. The real reason was that the blessing of a university label and medical school agreement would allow the charges for hospital services to increase. The hospital would be known as the North County University Hospital giving it a competitive edge over neighboring hospitals that did not have the sought-after university title. Like royalty and aristocracy, the medical staff rewarded with newly designed titles of academia could return the kingdom to the peace and riches of the past. That's what the accounting and finance departments of the hospital hoped for after spending millions of dollars on a consulting firm to research and sell the affiliation to the hospital board and doctors.

The chief of surgery and director of research, Doctor Hans Reisbach, had his career on the line due to recent cutbacks. He was one of a handful of surgeons in the country performing pancreatic transplant surgery to treat diabetes. Since it had been considered research, the operation wasn't fully reimbursed by private insurance, Medicaid or Medicare. The drug used to control rejection of the transplanted pancreas was developed by him and considered investigational, and the hospital was hoping to sell it to a pharmaceutical company after its approval by the Food and Drug Administration (FDA). Without a medical school arrangement and FDA approval, the drug would never make it to the marketplace in time to recover the money invested in its development. If the regulatory agency didn't approve the drug, it would die with Doctor Reisbach who dedicated his life to developing the medication and surgery and now was an old man.

Doctor Herbert Stark, Paul's boss and director of medicine was an arrogant man, with the unbridled hubris of his self-importance. He was backing Reisbach in the pursuit of the medical school affiliation. As a graduate of Ivy league schools, he was biased against most doctors who didn't have Ivy league credentials. A disturbing fact of life for him was his medical program which consisted of predominantly foreign medical school graduates. The truth was the program lacked the prestige to attract American graduates and, he desperately required the medical school affiliation to improve its standing.

Chapter Two

——————◆◆◆◆◆——————

P aul spent the afternoon in family court and on his way
home grabbed dinner at a local diner. Nothing was resolved
in court and the judge ordered them to seek counseling. He
was exhausted when he arrived at his apartment and decided
to get to bed much earlier than usual. Awakened by a phone
call at two AM, his first thought was that there was a problem
at the hospital and he hoped it could be resolved by telephone.
Although, he wasn't on call, the chief resident could call him
at any time of the day or night to help resolve difficulties
with the patients or staff. They often called him to be certain
they were doing the right thing and ran the problem by Paul
before calling a private patient's doctor. This saved the house
staff from the wrath of the private physican whose sleep was
interrupted by unnecessary queries about their patient in the
early morning hours. He was unprepared for the surprise call
from Raj's current wife Claudia who crying quietly told him
that Raj was in the emergency room.

Paul not fully awake asked, "What's he doing there?"

She said, "He was hit by a car while walking home from the hospital and was taken to the emergency room at the hospital."

She continued to tell him that he had been in the morgue all day reviewing Elaine's autopsy and decided to walk home that night to get some fresh air. Paul was speechless and couldn't believe what he was hearing.

He asked, "Is he is alright?" All he could hear was Claudia sobbing.

He looked at the clock and couldn't imagine why he had walked home at that hour after spending such a dreadful day in the morgue.

Paul rushed to the hospital to find that Raj was brought to the hospital, dead on arrival. Attempts to resuscitate him in the ambulance were unsuccessful. After learning that Raj had died, Paul could not muster the courage to look at his friends mangled body and said goodbye to his friend while standing next to his shrouded corpse. After wiping the tears away from his eyes, he returned to the ER waiting area to console Claudia. She seemed frightened and speaking in a barely audible voice appeared afraid of being overheard.

In a hushed tone, she whispered, "The hit and run was not an accident, it was deliberate."

Paul could see how distraught she was and didn't take her comment seriously.

He told her, "It's possible Raj was so troubled by Elaine's death that he just didn't see the car coming towards him."

She continued to voice her suspicion and trying to calm her, he said, "The deaths of Raj and Elaine on the same day are difficult to bear, and you need to be strong."

He realized her paranoia wasn't an unusual response to the overwhelming grief she was experiencing and delusions with incoherent speech could be expected. Paul had known her during the time she was married to Raj, and never saw her act out senselessly or irrationally. She had always impressed him as the school teacher type carrying herself with the air of authority and never appeared ruffled. For a level-headed lady, slim, petite and usually cool, calm and collected, her behavior seemed a bit strange. He realized that under the circumstances, her reaction was understandable although he never expected her to unravel as she had and was having trouble calming her down. He thought the din in the emergency room agitated her and asked the ER secretary to call a taxi for him to take her home.

To comfort her during the ride in the cab, he put his arm around her to rest her head on his shoulder. At home, she continued to cry uncontrollably, and he promised not to leave her alone. Feeling helpless, he asked if he could get her a cup of coffee.

She didn't answer and kept repeating, "Raj and Elaine were killed because they knew something terrible about the hospital that would destroy it."

She told Paul that Raj had been compiling the history of the local medical society and had difficulty finding background information on some of the doctors on the staff including the chief of surgery. Raj had told her that there was very little known about him prior to his medical training in Canada other than he had served as a young Luftwaffe pilot in Germany during World War Two. After the war, he escaped to Spain and afterwards emigrated to Argentina where he obtained a medical degree. He could not find any history of the Reisbach family or anything else about his life in Germany or South America except that there was a brother who had died during the war. She also mentioned that Elaine was having difficulty in her new position at the hospital. Raj was concerned about it however Claudia didn't know what the problem was.

He didn't understand what Reisbach's history or Elaine's problems in her new role at the hospital had to do with their deaths and told Claudia that her grief was getting the best of her. Afraid that she was heading for a complete mental and physical breakdown, he asked if there was anything in the house she could take for sleep. Thinking, a ten-milligram dose of valium would probably calm her and make her sleep, he found a vial containing some tablets in a medicine cabinet in the bathroom. While searching for the valium, he could only think of returning to his apartment to get some sleep but didn't want to leave her alone in her fragile mental state. He didn't know if she had any family nearby or neighbors that could care for her and thought that a good night's sleep would reduce her anguish. He waited about twenty minutes for the pill to take effect.

During that time, she mumbled, "The house was broken into a couple of weeks ago."

Continuing to talk slowly, every syllable became more slurred with time and he couldn't decipher what she was saying. Attempting to stay awake, she began nodding and finally fell asleep on the couch. Paul covered her with a blanket and left the house.

He decided to walk back to the hospital since his car was in the hospital parking lot and on his way back he found the spot where Raj was hit by the vehicle which was three blocks from Raj's home and equidistant from the hospital. The police had abandoned the scene of the accident by the time he arrived there and he looked for tire markings or blood stains that might explain how the accident happened. He questioned whether Raj stepped into the path of the car or the car had veered to hit him. The street lighting was bright, and it showed tire markings extending to the curb that curved outward from the center of the road indicating that the car had swerved. There were a few blood stains remaining that followed the tire tracks away from the curb, suggesting that the car had dragged Raj's body. Despite witnessing the markings of the tragedy that surrounded him, the cool early morning breeze felt good and he could appreciate why his friend decided to walk home that night. Although sleepy and exhausted, he was now suspicious that the car had been driven directly into Raj and then turned back towards the road. In his mind, it still didn't explain if it was a deliberate act or the result of the driver's loss of control while falling asleep or intoxicated from alcohol or drugs. It didn't look like Raj had walked far from the curb into the lane of a passing car and Paul began to think that maybe Claudia's suspicion required further scrutiny. Needing to clear his mind of all the conflicting thoughts and emotions, he continued his walk to the hospital where he decided to sleep and would think more about it in the morning. Exhausted, he didn't think he was alert enough to drive home and pictured himself lying on a cold slab next to his friend in the morgue after falling asleep at the wheel. Finding an empty bed in the house staff quarters, he was too tired to change into scrubs, and fell asleep in his street clothing. Feeling as though he had just fallen asleep, he had a rude awakening by Stark his chief of medicine at eight AM. In time for the morning conference and after a change into scrubs, he had breakfast in the chief's office.

In an attempt to make sense of the deaths of Raj and Elaine, he began discussing what he had experienced with Stark and the director of pathology, Doctor Herman Stern.

He said, "Claudia told me their home was burglarized a few weeks ago and she suspects that Raj's death was staged to look like a hit and run accident, but he was murdered."

Both chiefs scoffed at the idea and told him not to believe any of it. They explained it as obviously a distraught wife being somewhat delusional. Paul told them about the tire tracks and blood on the road at the scene of the accident. Appearing puzzled, they warned him not to get involved or discuss it with anyone in the hospital. They cautioned that if reporters and the newspapers got wind of the speculation about the deaths, it would ruin the prospect of a university affiliation for the hospital. They insisted that Elaine's death was due to dealing drugs even though Paul told them that Raj was adamant that she absolutely did not abuse drugs and had no financial reason to sell drugs.

Stern related, "Elaine's post mortem blood analysis was positive for ketamine and oxycodone and fresh needle marks were found on her body consistent with recent injections."

Convinced that Raj's death was accidental Stern added, "He should have had better sense than to walk home at that hour. The police report suggested a probable drunk driver and they are looking for the car. When they find the driver, it will prove they were right."

Paul sat there taking it all in and couldn't believe their smug responses to what he had told them. He could only think how demeaning it was to listen to their arrogant assumptions. Baffled by their reckless explanations of the two-deaths, they had treated him like a fool. Disgusted by the conversation and having difficulty controlling his anger, he stormed out of the office desperately seeking someone to speak with and get it off his chest. He called his wife Maria, who was shocked and saddened by the news of Raj and Elaine's deaths. After a few empathizing words, she advised Paul to quit working at the hospital and return to his former medical practice in the Bronx.

She responded, "You belong in the South Bronx where you can help people without dealing with the insanity of hospital politics."

He should have known better than to call his wife and realized that asking for her support was a mistake and predictably discomforting. Now that Raj was gone, he believed he had no one to confide in and discuss his inner most feelings with. Following the futile conversation with Maria, and with his unresolved anger, he hurried to finish rounds and left the hospital to find some peace and solace in his apartment.

Chapter Three

————◆————

P aul entered the apartment angered and agitated from the futile meeting and his wife's exasperating negativity. Overwhelmed with hostility and bursting with pent up frustration, he desperately needed someway to relax before he kicked in a wall or someone's butt. Never in the habit of drinking alcohol during the day, he searched in the kitchen cupboard and discovered a bottle of scotch whiskey that was given to him by a grateful patient. Pouring a stiff drink and gulping it down, he quickly poured another as his furor rose and fumed about his boss and Stern. The way they talked about his friends, treating them as though they were disposable syringes, used, wasted and then thrown out in a hazardous waste bin infuriated him.

After Raj had migrated to the USA, he was employed by Stern as his personal, professional slave. Raj was grateful to Stern for offering him a job and the opportunity to become an American citizen. Without family in the United States, the hospital was his surrogate home, and he was loyal to it. Doing most of Stern's work while paid much less than other pathologists in the city and reaching no recognition for his job, he ran the entire lab, providing the required conferences and supervision of the laboratory staff. Stern advanced his career by hobnobbing with hospital administrators and with the prospect of a university affiliation was seldom seen in the hospital while spending time in the medical school kissing professorial butt. Paul didn't receive much better treatment by Stark who enjoyed ridiculing him, with the remark that without affirmative action, he would have never been accepted to medical school. The administration and hospital board knew about the abusive treatment both physicians received and chose to ignore it. They dismissed it as going with the turf and medical pecking order.

With more contempt and bitterness, he gulped down another shot of whiskey and dozed off on the couch. He hadn't slept more than twenty minutes when the phone rang. As he slowly aroused from his stupor, his answering machine recorded the call, and all he heard was something about a detective at the hospital. He wasn't fully awake and thought it was a dream. Shaking his head to sober up, as his alcoholic haze began to lift, he reached for the playback button on the machine to hear the call from the hospital staff office about a detective wanting to speak to him. He wasn't sure he was ready to speak to the police while he was half in the bag and after brewing coffee downed a couple of cups. When he thought he was sufficiently clear headed, he called the hospital. The staff secretary told him an FBI agent was looking for him and gave him a number to call. Questioning why the FBI was investigating the auto accident, he immediately dialed the number. A woman answered saying she was agent Karen

Andersen and with his mind continuing in a fog from the alcohol, he couldn't imagine a woman FBI agent. She spoke with a rapid, clipped military cadence of a drill sergeant and wanted to see him immediately. He told her he was in his apartment and gave her the address.

While waiting and wondering about the call, he worried why she was questioning him and if she had interviewed other people at the hospital who knew as much or more of what had happened than he did. His head was throbbing with a pounding headache and he wasn't in a frame of mind for questioning by the FBI or anyone else. The doorbell rang, and he reluctantly went to open the door. As he opened it, he was met by a gorgeous gal with flowing blonde hair and a fantastic body. Still under the influence of the liquor, believing there was some mistake and she had the wrong apartment, he asked if he could help her. Andersen was puzzled by the question but disregarded it and introduced herself. Feeling like a fool, recovering from his drunken inertia, he invited her in and apologized for the messy apartment, offered her a chair, and asked if she wanted something to drink. He couldn't take his eyes off her and continued to stare.

Curious about his strange introduction she asked, "Is there a problem?"

Without thinking, he said, "I didn't know there were female FBI agents."

What he really meant to say but remained unsaid was, "I didn't know there were women in the FBI as beautiful as you."

Getting the gist of what he meant, she flashed her badge and remarked, "Apparently you don't get to watch much television."

He saw that her credentials were those of an FBI special agent and wanted to ask her what the difference was between a regular agent and one that was special. However, after starting off lamely on the wrong foot and feeling like an idiot, he kept his mouth shut and let her do the talking. After she had explained why she was there, he wanted to know if she had spoken to other employees at the hospital. She answered she had not.

Baffled by her answer and with a bewildered facial expression, he paused awhile before asking, "Why me?"

She explained that after investigating the personal histories of all the employees at the hospital including the physicians on the staff, he was the one most closely linked to the two dead people. Without further thought, he revealed the chain of events including his and Claudia's suspicions and the chiefs' lack of interest in the murders of two key employees. Reassured he would cooperate, she told him that she wanted to meet with him the following day after she had a chance to review some of the information he had given her. To protect his job, he didn't wish to be seen talking to an FBI agent, and insisted that they meet at a location far from the hospital. She agreed and suggested that he pick the place.

Chapter Four

A fraid of being seen, he chose a Mexican restaurant in New York's Spanish Harlem. When he informed her of the location, she told him that she wasn't from New York or staying in the city and didn't know her way around Manhattan. She had asked him for detailed directions and he realized the FBI was using an agent from out of town rather than one from New York. Waiting at the rear of the restaurant seated in a dingy red booth of faux leather, he nervously tapped his fingers on the table trying to figure out why the FBI hadn't used an agent from New York. He was determined to get an answer as soon as she arrived.

Constantly scanning the entrance of the restaurant and its store front window facing Third Avenue, he impatiently awaited her arrival. Through the large window, the interior of the restaurant was plainly visible to pedestrians passing-by. Nevertheless, he was confident that no one who knew him would eat there or stroll by and believed it was the perfect location for a clandestine meeting. The ambiance had all the components of a greasy spoon with old faded posters of scenic Mexico, dusty sombreros and cheap decorations hung on the walls that completed its dingy appearance. Despite the rundown appearance, one of the nurses at the hospital had suggested it as an inexpensive casual spot with good Mexican food. After sitting there for a while and noticing the tables with their frayed and stained red and white checkered tablecloths, he had doubts about eating there. Maria, his wife would have found it disgusting and would have refused to eat there and he wondered if the gorgeous FBI agent would feel the same way. He was curious about the agent's reaction, but it was too late to change the venue and find another place to eat.

She entered the restaurant, and immediately spotted him in the dark corner booth. Flustered from trying to find a parking space in the city, she couldn't understand why he had picked such a seedy place to meet far from the hospital. In that part of town, finding a parking space on a main thoroughfare close to the restaurant was an impossible task. She thought she would need to display her government parking permit on the car's dashboard to park in a restricted space but after circling several blocks found a legal spot on a side street several blocks from the restaurant. The area had all the makings of a war zone with crumbling buildings surrounded by rubble and she wondered if the car would still be there when she returned.

The irritation of dealing with Paul was evident on her face as she entered the restaurant with her mouth rigidly clenched and lips tightly pursed. From where he was seated, he could see her tousled hair and pouting lips, and thought she looked very sexy. With a better look at her face as she sat down across from him, he recognized that she was upset and apologized for not finding a better place to meet.

Maintaining her cool, she politely said, "That's okay, it's nice."

She asked him if he had eaten there often and what he recommended from the menu. Embarrassed that he had never been there before, he avoided a direct answer and stated everything on the menu was great. Nervously thumbing through the menu, he waited, hesitating for an appropriate moment to ask why the FBI had chosen her, an out of town agent, to investigate the New York deaths.

As she observed his fidgeting and shuffling through the menu, she asked, "Is there anything wrong?"

Her question came at the right time for him to ask her "Why isn't the FBI using a New York agent to solve local murders and where are you from?"

After some thought, her explanation was that she had been asked to reopen a case involving several deaths of hospital employees in Idaho when Doctor Reisbach was director of transplant surgery there. The New York and Idaho deaths taken alone were unusual especially since the dead were all medical personnel who had lived and worked in distant areas of the country and had a connection with the same surgeon at two different hospitals. Although a couple of murders were not uncommon in the greater New York area, the cluster of several deaths occurring in a similar setting in a geographically distant small Idaho community showed up on the FBI's radar and compelled them to further investigate them.

She paused as the waiter took their order for burritos with salsa verde and side dishes of refried beans and guacamole. While waiting to be served, he wanted to know why she was recruited to investigate the deaths in Idaho. She explained that she had grown up in the county in Idaho where they occurred and was familiar with the community and the people. Her father was a pharmacist who had worked for Reisbach at the hospital. He was one of the victims and was killed while fishing in a local lake by what was believed at the time to be a hunter's stray bullet. The perpetrator was never identified and after three more employees of the same hospital died mysteriously, there was suspicion that her father's death may not have been an accident. No solid evidence of foul play was ever uncovered however, the causes of deaths continue to be suspicious.

Obsessed with finding her father's killer, after college, she sought a position with the FBI and was accepted as a trainee agent. One of her first assignments included the investigation of the suspicious deaths in her hometown. Fervent about finding closure for her father's death, agent Andersen confided that it was personal, and not just government business.

The impassioned remark that revealed her compelling motive wasn't the usual tough cop talk that he had expected and was surprisingly appealing. Her candidness about her personal involvement took the edge out of the meeting and he felt flattered that she would disclose her personal feelings to him. Even though Reisbach was associated with the hospitals in both states, he didn't understand how the surgeon could be tied to the deaths and told her that he doubted the respected physician had anything to do with them. Shaking his head in disbelief, Paul was stunned by her assertions about the surgeon. He told her that Reisbach was a pioneer in organ transplantation surgery and had been honored with awards for his efforts to cure diabetes with pancreatic transplants, published hundreds of scientific papers and held memberships in highly respected medical societies and foundations which listed him on their boards.

As they were finishing dessert, she dropped the sixty-four-million-dollar question, "Do you think you can help me with the investigation?"

Without hesitating, he answered, "Of course, any help you need."

She explained that she needed inside information from hospital employees who were reluctant to talk to an FBI agent but would not have difficulty talking about the same things with a respected physician on the staff. The problem that Elaine was having in her new job with the surgical department and what Raj knew about Reisbach and the hospital that frightened his wife were some of the questions he could help get answered.

She understood Paul's skepticism about the chief of surgery's possible involvement, however, his help could resolve some of the doubts about the surgeon. As she continued with her account, he was unprepared for what followed next when she confirmed that she had studied Reisbach's medical career and was convinced that he had lied about his identity and wasn't who he pretended to be. To be certain about it required further digging into his family history and finding out more about his twin brother who was missing during World War Two and believed killed but his body was never recovered. She told him that his help would be needed to establish Reisbach's past criminal history if the recent murders weren't solved and that could involve some travel on his part.

Dumbfounded and openmouthed, he didn't know what to say as he sat there awaiting a further explanation.

After a silence longer than a few seconds, he stammered, "Where?"

Hesitating in a low voice, she replied "It might involve travel to Europe and possibly South America."

Ridiculous, he thought and loudly protested stumbling on his words asking, "Why would I and what makes you think I could do that or would want to?"

Looking straight into his eyes she said, "To document that the murders attributed to Reisbach started long before those suspected in the States and using his brother's identity he has covered up his past crimes that were committed during the Second World War. To locate his brother or brother's family in Europe who can identify him as a murdering war criminal and not the former Luftwaffe pilot who he claims to have been."

Shocked, he couldn't believe or understand what he had heard and stammered, "I can't leave the country! It is out of the question!"

It would jeopardize his job and the divorce, he bellowed, "Stark would never allow me to leave the country to help the FBI solve a crime and my wife would make the divorce more unbearably impossible!"

He became furious that he had promised to help her and felt that she had hoodwinked him into agreeing to help her with something he was unable to do.

Feeling misled, he emphatically said, "No!"

Seeing how agitated he had become, she calmly tried to explain that she could arrange to get time off from his job and help him resolve some of the problems with the divorce. His return to work was guaranteed, she emphasized.

"I have the power of the FBI backing me," she boasted.

Trying to recover from being a pushover, he said "I want a guarantee in writing."

She changed her tune and admitted it was impossible since there's no assurance to the outcome of the investigation and her superiors wouldn't approve of anything in writing under the circumstances. Explaining further that it was not FBI policy to provide written agreements to those who helped with an investigation, the answer would be a definite no.

Getting out of the booth, leaving her there sitting alone while he walked away, he roared "You must be nuts to think I'd drop everything I'm doing with a word of mouth proposal and a promise."

Unfazed by his outburst, she tried motivating him with guilt and said, "Why don't you consider it, after all, your best friend and his ex-wife were murdered, and you agreed to help me."

The remark agitated him more as he walked out of the restaurant repeating, "No way! No way!"

While driving back to Westchester, he mulled over the entire conversation at the restaurant and couldn't think of anything she'd say that would change his mind. Agitated and obsessing about the discussion, he needed to calm down and did something he had never done before. He called in sick and left the message with Stark's secretary that he wouldn't be returning to the hospital that afternoon. Having guilt about lying that he was sick, he began feeling remorseful about refusing to help with the investigation of Elaine and Raj's deaths.

Chapter Five

Unable to sleep, Paul was out of bed early the next morning and called in sick again. Struggling with indecision about cooperating with Andersen's investigation, unable to concentrate on his work and resolve the quandary that was plaguing him, Raj's death depressed him further. He missed talking to his dead friend and knew that if he were alive, he would've helped him make the right decision. A long walk occasionally helped him think more clearly however he was stuck in the apartment awaiting the expected call from Stark who would want to know why he wasn't at the hospital. If he didn't answer, it would blow his excuse. Languishing there, futilely wishing the business with the FBI would magically vanish like a bad dream, his anguish deepened with the realization that Andersen would also call. The phone rang and waiting for the answering machine to begin recording before he'd pick it up, it was Stark's voice, and he quickly answered. Stark was curt and told him to report to work unless he was severely ill. Calling in sick, complicated things and he should have known Stark wouldn't let him get away with a lame excuse. Sheepishly, Paul admitted that he wasn't ill and quickly contrived the story that his father was sick, and his mother was distraught and had been calling him all morning for medical advice.

Stark barked, "Well, bring him to the hospital, and I'll have someone examine him!"

Paul replied, "That's difficult, my dad's in Puerto Rico."

"Do whatever you have to do and get back to work!" Stark answered and hung up.

The phone rang again, and Paul took the call.

It was Karen Andersen who very meekly said, "I owe you an apology for the way I pressured you yesterday."

Ignoring her attempt to appease him, he heatedly answered, "What do you want?

She said, "I called the hospital, and they told me you were sick. Rather than discussing it on the phone, I'll come to your apartment."

To avoid her, he replied, "You shouldn't come here, I've got an intestinal bug, and furthermore I have nothing to discuss with you."

"Was it the Mexican food?" she asked

He finished the call with her, and within what seemed like a few minutes, she was knocking on his door. As soon as he opened it, she knew immediately that he wasn't sick.

She joked, "You seem to have recovered quickly."

He mumbled, "The medicine seems to be working."

Wheedling him, she smugly replied, "We ate the same food, and I didn't get sick."

Dropping the pretense, he told her that he didn't wish to see her, and he was not cooperating with her investigation.

He said, "Stark had just called and wanted me to go to the hospital to be examined. I couldn't get away with that story, so I made up another that my mother was worried about my dad who was very sick, and I'd been on the phone with her all morning."

Seeing how upset he appeared, she asked, "Is your father seriously ill?"

Raising his voice, he insisted that no one was sick, "They're all lies to attempt to isolate myself until I resolve how to justify not helping to find my friends' killers without feeling guilty."

Following the outburst, he explained that his father had prostate cancer but has been doing well since his surgery.

He recounted, "Stark wanted me to take him to the hospital, and that was not possible since dad lives in Puerto Rico."

Dispirited and visibly exhausted, he said, "I'm sick of all the deception and manipulation and refuse to get involved with your scheme that would only disrupt my life more than it is now."

Shifting gears and changing the course of the conversation to appear sympathetic, she advised that it might be the time for him take a break and use the investigation to stall and drag out the divorce proceeding until all the emotion and drama of it waned. She admitted that she also had gone through a bitter divorce that eventually worked out with time.

He said his wife would continue to harass him no matter how he tried to evade dealing with her or the divorce. Furthermore, asking Stark to give him time to help her uncover a possible connection between the murders and the hospital was out of the question, since Stark believed the deaths had nothing to do with the hospital

He added, "You're asking me to commit suicide because that's what getting involved with your scheme would be for me."

Thinking aloud she said, "Maybe you could use your father's illness as a way to get a leave of absence?"

Looking at her with an expression that questioned her sanity, he made it clear that his father's cancer had been removed, and he was not dying.

"They don't know that?" she exclaimed! "He couldn't refuse you if you told him your father was in hospice."

Appalled by her suggestion, he became irate and shouted, "I can't lie about that. He's not dying, and I would never state that he was near death!"

Although he appeared angered, she thought of a way that might change his mind, and the hospital couldn't refuse family leave and said, "The FBI could make his medical records appear as though your father was seriously ill, and near death."

She reasoned, "You are an only child, and leaving your elderly mother alone in Puerto Rico to care for your father while he's dying would be terrible. What better excuse do you need?"

He seemed visibly disturbed by the deception she was plotting to use for a family leave of absence about his father's cancer. Although thinking about getting his wife and the divorce proceedings out of his life, even for a while, was sounding good, he wouldn't admit that to her.

Paul nervously paced the floor vehemently replying, "I can't lie about that. It's offensive and painful for me to say someone was at death's door when they were not and especially about one as close and personal as my father."

Though he hated the pretext, he had no qualms about escaping from all the hassling about the divorce which seemed to soften him on the idea of using his father's health. Continuing the pressure, she repeated that the bureau could provide his father's revised medical records in a day or two and a phone number registered in Puerto Rico that could be answered from anywhere in the world. She explained the need for the phone number since Stark might call Puerto Rico periodically to check on his whereabouts and the condition of his father while they were in Europe looking for Reisbach's twin brother.

Totally confused and seething with indignation he insisted, "I told you I'm not going to South America, Europe or any other country with you."

She was determined to convince him that the surgeon wasn't who he claimed to be and had a twin brother who had lived and could still be alive in Europe. Reisbach was a murderer responsible for deaths not only in the States but also in Auschwitz concentration camp in Poland during World War Two.

Shaking his head mocking her, he said, "I don't believe that about him and trying to find his brother who had been missing since World War Two would be futile and frankly a dumb idea. Considering Doctor Reisbach's age, even if the twin has been missing all the while, he'd probably be dead by now."

"Searching for the brother was crazier than looking for a needle in a haystack." He derided and continued, "Why do you need me for digging up Reisbach's or his brother's past when the FBI has plenty of agents to do that?"

To convince him, she elaborated on how accompanying her, would be a big help. Looking for a war criminal, former Nazi or a Second World War army deserter in Europe and asking about their role during the war, was not something an FBI agent would get much cooperation with. Calmly she tried to explain that what happened during the war continued to be a sensitive issue in some European countries. Notably, that generation avoided any discussion of it with outsiders and was very secretive about the Nazi war period. A physician traveling with his secretary gathering information for a biography of a famous surgeon born in Germany would seem relatively non-threatening and inspire dialogue that an FBI agent could never obtain. Cajoling him, she added doctors were more highly regarded in Europe than in the USA.

"Moreover, you're Hispanic, and Spain could be the starting point for our investigation," she stressed.

He was still puzzled about all the places she talked about from phone calls to Puerto Rico, travel to Europe and now Spain.

"Why Spain if he's German?" he demanded.

Patiently continuing with her line of reasoning, she informed him that many Germans had escaped to Spain and Argentina during and after the war. Those countries were sympathetic to Germany, and the Nazis did business with them and traveled freely within them. She admitted that her mother was born in Germany and taught her German as a child. Now as an adult she could still get by speaking it but that would spark suspicion of her motive for asking sensitive questions in Spain or Germany. Besides, she hadn't spoken German since her mother died many years before. He made it clear to her that his ability to speak the Puerto Rican variety of Spanish was limited and added that it wasn't the same as the Spanish spoken in Spain.

"That's good enough," was her swift irate response.

"What's so important about traveling out of the country to document that Doctor Reisbach was the evil brother. Can't you just pin the murders here in the States on him and get it over with?" he goaded her.

Sensing his enormous resistance, she began to question whether trying to persuade him was worth the effort. The murders in New York could represent her last opportunity to catch Reisbach since there was never enough evidence to tie him to the suspected killings in Idaho. She was determined to persist and establish his past identity by uncovering the history in Poland during the world war and connect it to the murders in the States, putting him in prison for life. Her patience explaining all this to Paul was rapidly dissipating and with her face flushed, feeling as though at any moment she would lose it, she struggled to keep calm. She explained that during World War Two, he was a suspected war criminal who had experimented on and killed Jews and others in Auschwitz concentration camp. He had worked with the infamous Doctor Mengele. She said, Mengele, had a strange interest in studying the physical traits of twins and made him his assistant because he knew Reisbach, a twin would help recruit subjects.

"Reisbach couldn't have been a doctor then. He would be over a hundred years old now if he were a physician at that time!" Paul exclaimed.

She asserted that he was only a student preparing to study medicine and at the time hadn't finished his premedical studies. He didn't need a medical degree to commit atrocities while working with Doctor Mengele.

Catching his interest, he was curious about how she found out Reisbach was associated with Mengele.

"How do you know that? he asked.

Karen Andersen had grown up in northern Idaho in a predominantly German community. There were many rumors about Reisbach's role at Auschwitz and the torture and deaths in the concentration camp. His role during the war was often a topic of the gossip in the Idaho community where he was on the surgical staff of the hospital. It was one of the issues that eventually made him leave Idaho.

The hospital and medical school there couldn't substantiate the rumors, but when hospital personnel began to die mysteriously, and murder was suspected, he resigned and left town. The medical center and university never publicly disclosed the reason behind his resignation and departure from the state and kept it as their dirty little secret. He departed with excellent recommendations from the hospital and medical school in Idaho. However, he couldn't find a similar position elsewhere in a university hospital setting and as a result, ended up at North County Hospital in New York. The hospital board and administration ignored the rumors and suspicions at that time. They were interested in him since his research in pancreatic transplantation was at the forefront of the surgical treatment of diabetes and his presence would enhance the medical center's reputation in the medical community.

To win Paul over to her plan, she realized that he knew very little about the history preceding or during the World War Two era and she mercilessly plied him with more information trying to convince him of the importance of his role. Having taught high school history before her acceptance to the FBI, she structured the conversation as a lecture and decided to enlighten him with a thing or two about it.

Amazed, she asked, "Hadn't you learned of Hitler's obsession with eugenics and the Aryan race?"

"Genetics?" he asked, thinking she had mispronounced the word.

"No eugenics," she raised her voice.

She couldn't believe he didn't seem to distinguish the difference between eugenics and genetics. Stressing that many well-respected academic circles before and during World War Two, had considered it science because some scientists had proposed racial and ethnic theories that were determined from physical traits, and it became popular. The Nazis adopted it and loved those ideas using them to allege that the Jews, had many characteristics that were responsible for Germany's failures after World War One. She emphasized eugenics was a phony discipline, and later called a pseudoscience which continued to be accepted by many individuals after that period even in the United States. Nothing of any scientific or humanitarian value was derived from it and the theories were used as the rationale for many evil things. At the time, criminality, insanity, low intelligence, poor work habits and a slew of other social problems were attributed to the notions derived from eugenics. In this country, it was used to discriminate against any minority that didn't fit the white Anglo-Saxon ideal. This included most immigrants and all Jews and African-Americans. Getting heated, she continued that right in New York on Long Island, there was a Bureau of Eugenics funded by some of America's most reputable and wealthiest families. The ideas promoted there were praised by the Nazis, and many were applied by them to justify their horrible crimes. The assistant director of the laboratory there was honored and awarded medals by Hitler. She continued, the same institution later became world famous for its research on the human gene and cancer. He couldn't believe that early in its history, the laboratory on the north shore of Long Island had played a part in the eugenics movement.

Surprised that he hadn't learned of it during his training as a doctor, she exclaimed, "I cannot believe you never learned this in medical school."

"Why in medical school?" he wanted to know.

Raising her voice, "Weren't you required to take courses in medical ethics?"

He didn't know how to answer and wasn't sure what she expected him to say.

Shrugging his shoulders, he flippantly said, "What do you expect, I went to a city college and medical school?"

She was getting testy but tried to lighten things up by remarking that he may have fallen asleep during those lectures. He shrugged his shoulders as if to ask why do you care? Despite trying to interest him further about the project, she seemed not to be gaining much ground. Exploring a technique that she had learned at the agency, she embellished her strategy using little-known material that might arouse his interest.

She related the story that Reisbach and Mengele fled to Argentina around the same time and probably were friends. While Reisbach was going to medical school in Buenos Aires, Mengele owned a drug or chemical company there that produced various types of chemicals and drugs which he peddled as vitamins. Some believed them to be weird medicines that could change the physical characteristics of the human body which was consistent with his interest in studying the physical traits and genetics of twins. It was said that he wanted to breed twins to build an Aryan race. Reisbach seems to have gotten some of his ideas for the anti-rejection drugs from Mengele that he later developed for transplant surgery. While attending medical school in Buenos Aires, he worked for Mengele to make money to support himself and likely shared ideas with him about the drugs that were being manufactured.

Adding more fuel to the story, she continued, "There were stories documented in FBI files of people identifying Hitler in Argentina at the same time."

Expressing amazement, he said, "That can't be? Hitler committed suicide, and his burned corpse was found with a bullet hole in its skull by the Russians at the end of the war."

She retorted, "That appears to have been refuted by DNA tests of the skull. The DNA was identified as that from a woman's skull and couldn't have been Hitler's."

Amazed, all he could say was, "They actually did a DNA analysis of it."

Now she had his attention and continued. Hitler stayed in an area of Argentina called Cordoba and was hidden from international Nazi hunters by Argentinians who were Nazis.

The FBI had eyewitness reports of sightings of Hitler while he was there. Mengele who had changed his name while in Buenos Aires was exposed by the Israelis and fled to Brazil. He lived in a remote location near a jungle town in southern Brazil called Candido Godoi posing as a doctor hired by the Brazilian government to improve the local health care for women especially prenatal care. In his mind, it was the ideal setting for the creation of a new Nazi race. The original settlers in the town were Germans who had been there before World War Two, and the women from the village had experienced a high rate of infant deaths and miscarriages which were unusual in healthy German women. The population that had settled there had a variety of physical characteristics, but many had Aryan physical features with blue eyes and blonde hair. Mengele impersonating a doctor studying reproductive health found it to be the perfect location for his experiments.

Visiting the town weekly, he examined fertile women interested in starting families and had no difficulty cultivating a following with his fluent German and warm German charm. Not too long after he had begun his medical care of the women, there was a surge in multiple births. Most of them were twins with blond hair and blue eyes and typical Aryan features. Although many of the children were sets of twins from unrelated families, the physical similarities of those from different mothers were incredibly unreal and striking.

Paul was dumbfounded and asked, "Did he impregnate all those women?"

No, it would have been impossible for him to be the father of all those children and besides he didn't have the typical Aryan physical attributes that could be passed on to another generation, Karen Andersen replied. He would go to the village regularly to examine the women, draw blood for testing and then gave them pills.

Paul skeptical demanded, "What kind of pills?"

She said the townspeople called them vitamins and they were happy that Doctor Mengele provided them for free. The women there stopped having miscarriages, and infant deaths were no longer a problem. They began producing healthy German babies with almost identical Aryan features. Paul thought the story was a fairy tale and asked for proof that it actually had happened. She said even today the town's women often give birth to twins and children with similar physical appearances. The elderly villagers continue to claim that a German doctor after the war had regularly attended to the women's health in their town.

Protesting he said, "I don't believe any of it. To do this, he would have had to somehow change the DNA of the young women he supposedly treated. Even today no one has developed a drug that can do that."

She replied, "If you don't believe me, Google it. Newspaper articles have been written about it, and there was even a book and movie based on it."

Eventually, the Brazilian government discovered that he was there, and he fled to Paraguay where many years later he died of natural causes. It's been said that Hitler was also seen in Brazil, not that far from where Mengele was hiding. Maybe he and Mengele were planning a fourth Reich. The story was that both fled from Argentina and Brazil when war criminals began to be hunted. About that time, Reisbach had graduated from medical school in Buenos Aires and with foreign agents chasing Nazi war criminals, he applied and was accepted to a surgical residency program at a hospital in Canada.

Paul wanted to know why with all the information known on Reisbach, they hadn't arrested him. To answer, she replied that he used his twin brother's identity and claimed he wasn't the guy who worked with Mengele in the concentration camp. The authorities could never prove otherwise because the brother had disappeared and was never traced. Using someone else's identity even without having a twin was easy after the war. People died, their bodies never found, and others just vanished without proof of being dead or alive.

Sarcastically, she said, "I'll bet you never learned any of this in history class when you were in school."

Noting the sarcasm, he replied, "Growing up in the Bronx I was an excellent student graduating from parochial school with honors and at the top of my class."

"Did you ever explore the world beyond the Bronx?" she teased.

"You know you're a smart ass," he blasted.

My father and mother owned a bodega and worked sixteen hours a day from Monday to Sunday to live the American dream and pay for my schooling. There wasn't time to explore museums or money for anything but the essentials. The television was our cultural gateway, and the Bronx Zoo was the only foreign travel, we could afford, as he responded with a sour smile.

Not convinced that anyone in New York City could have had such a limited life, she pried further and asked about college and medical school. The experience was similarly constrained by commuting to college and medical school by bus and subway. After traveling, he helped his parents in the store, studied and went to bed. She wanted to know how he met his wife and Paul explained that they attended the same school and knew each other from the second or third grade.

What she heard saddened her and she stopped grilling him. Though she came from a small town in Idaho, she had experienced more of life than he described. It was pitiful, but she thought it explained his personality. Not seeming to have any regrets about what he revealed, it was his version of a fulfilled life. Her thought was that what he had portrayed was merely existing and compared to her norms, not living. To not upset him, she didn't comment on his life story, but it gave her a good idea of who she had chosen to work with.

Chapter Six

———◆·◆·◆———

Paul Peres hated imposters who paraded themselves as honorable men and were not held accountable for their transgressions. Karen Andersen's plea for help to investigate the murders that followed Reisbach's footprints but were never directly linked to him hurled Paul's life into a turmoil that was ripping him apart. The confusion and chaos created by his divorce and medical career paralyzed his sense of duty to expose the person or persons believed to be responsible for the deaths of his colleague and friends, and now he had to find the courage and determination to render justice for them.

The following day Paul showed up early for the morning conference in the chief's office, and then made hospital rounds with the residents. He returned to Stark's office to talk to him in private. His boss greeted him with usual sarcasm and asked him if his father had recovered from the illness that kept him on the phone with his mother and out of the hospital the preceding day. The unsettling awareness of Stark's hostile persona and chilling distant facial expression magnified by an icy mustache and goatee on his pale white face convinced Paul to be direct about proposing his leave of absence. He told his boss that he had spent the prior day speaking to his mother and his dad's doctor and demanded a leave of absence for a couple weeks to care for his father who was dying of cancer.

The chief's agitated face suddenly turned bright red, accentuating its snow-white facial hair while he choked on his words to say, "You're nuts!"

Stark rose from his chair and pounding a tightly clenched fist on the desk screamed, "Do you really believe I'm demented and would allow you to do that?"

He continued to yell, "You know what the situation is around here! We're short staffed, low on funds and can't function with a physician gone that long. I can't just pick up a phone and call a temp agency for a replacement?"

Paul was defiant and calmly said, "I thought you'd react this way, so I'm going to human resources and request compassionate leave with or without your approval. Legally, they must give it to me."

Stammering, Stark sputtered, "Don't think you're coming back here when you return. You'll be lucky to get a job cleaning floors in this town when I'm done with you."

"We'll see," said Paul as he slammed the door behind him.

He rushed to the personnel office, filled out the paperwork and promised to return with a doctor's report documenting his father's condition. Walking out of the office, finally realizing what he had done, he suddenly became shaky and sick to his stomach. How the hell am I going to explain all of this to my parents and my soon to be ex-wife he wondered? He hastily returned to the afternoon clinic and prepared the residents and interns to function without him and returned home.

He called FBI agent Andersen with a message threatening that he'd change his mind if she didn't have his father's medical records for his leave of absence that she had promised. With his head reeling, he decided to call his wife, and thought about how he would break the news about going to Puerto Rico to care for his sick father.

Surprised by the call she asked, "When did this happen?"

Remaining calm, he reminded her that his father had undergone surgery for prostate cancer, but it had not been completely removed and required further treatment. The disease was not responding to the medication and had gotten worse. She apparently believed him and quietly answered she was sorry to hear that, but in her characteristic style added that she hoped it wouldn't delay the divorce because she had to get on with her life.

Imploring her, he said, "Maria, I have no control over this, and at the most, it will only be a few weeks before I return. He will either improve or die!"

He couldn't believe how cold that sounded. However, it temporarily quieted her but didn't reassure him that it would completely satisfy her and not require that he continue to lie.

She said she would call his father to wish him well. Uncertain how to respond, he made the excuse that his mother was distraught, and it wasn't a good time to call. He asked her to wait until he arrived in Puerto Rico and assessed the situation before she spoke to his parents.

She agreed, but it was accompanied by a stinging reminder, "Be sure to see the kids before you go, they still think of you as their father!"

"Ok, I'll call to see them before I leave," he quickly said and hung up.

Relieved that she had accepted the story, he chose not to respond to the guilt-laden snipe about his relationship with the kids.

The phone rang, and it was Karen Andersen.

As his wife's bitter reply continued to rankle him, he abruptly replied, "What do you want?"

Surprised by his fiery greeting, she paused before explaining that she had spoken to Raj's wife about reviewing the history of the medical society and the biographical material on Reisbach that Raj had been working on at home. Claudia had agreed to show it to Karen, only if Paul accompanied her to the house.

"When can you get over there with me?" Karen asked.

He threatened her, "When you get the damn medical records to me for the alibi for my leave."

"I can't get them that fast, or waste time waiting for them before we gather information, so, we must see Claudia tonight," she commanded.

They bantered back and forth.

Challenging her, he struck back and said, "Well, I can't take the time until the leave is approved."

Insisting, she wanted to know, "What about tonight, do you need a doctor's note for that?"

Pissed off, he worried aloud, "Look, I can't fully commit to this unless I have some documentation that what I'm about to do has been approved by the FBI. Those phony medical records are my proof, and without them, I have nothing to fall back on if your scheme fails."

"Don't fret, I'll take care of it," was her response.

"How and when?" he shouted.

Feeling guilty about his lack of resolve to help on Raj's behalf, he agreed to meet her there at eight PM. Karen couldn't believe how he attempted to back down after accepting to help her.

Still, in a quandary about how to address the subject of family leave with his parents and his visit to Puerto Rico, he called them. His mother answered, and in a somewhat subdued voice, he indicated that he was taking some time off from work in the coming week to see them. She was surprised and told him it was great news, adding that his father would be overjoyed to see him. She sensed from the drone in his voice that he wasn't as happy about the trip as he should be.

"Are you taking the kids?" his mother asked.

He replied. "Mom you know under the circumstances, Maria won't let that happen."

His mother volunteered to call Maria to ask her to bring the children.

"Ma, please, don't do that! It's tough taking the kids out of school." He stressed, "You know how difficult she's become during the divorce."

Not wanting to hound him, she told him that he had made her day. The call was more comfortable than he thought it would be and finally, he began to relax.

Overwhelmed by the tension, he was sleepy and dozed off on the couch with the phone still in his hand. Falling into a deep sleep, the phone dropped from his hand between cushions on the sofa, and he didn't hear the buzzing noise the phone made while being disconnected. Startled by loud banging on his door, he awakened in a fog and shuffled to the door where he was greeted by Andersen.

Enraged she yelled, "What the hell is wrong with you? We were supposed to be at Claudia's house more than an hour ago, and your phone line has been busy all the while."

He explained that he had fallen asleep, and the phone must have become accidently disconnected.

She hollered, "You're not supposed to nap when there is something important to do, and I hope the phone wasn't purposely disconnected."

Groggy and not wanting to argue, he excused himself to pour cold water on his face and wake up. Karen drove with him to Raj's house, and as they walked up the entrance steps, they saw the door ajar.

"What the hell is going on?" Paul asked.

Karen thought that Claudia left the door unlocked for them.

Paul answered, "Not in New York. No one leaves doors unlocked or open!"

They rushed into the house calling out Claudia's name several times with no reply. Walking towards the kitchen, they passed the library with books strewn all over the floor, desk draws open and papers scattered all around them. Moving into the kitchen, Karen carrying her gun in her hand ran up the back stairs to the second floor while Paul hurriedly searched through the first floor. She returned, and they both went down to Raj's office in the basement. They encountered the same mess as in the library with file cabinets opened, a desk overturned, file folders and papers thrown everywhere, and yet there was no sign of her.

Up the steps to the backyard, they stopped in their tracks at the sight of Claudia, dead with her body hanging from the clothesline and her head dangling with the line tightly twisted around her neck. Her face was blue and swollen with eyes protruding out of their sockets. Paul horrified, turned and vomited. Terrified by her eyes staring blindly at him created an immediate flashback to his waking dead nightmares.

He cried out, "That F---ing bastard!"

Karen appalled by what was done to Claudia, grabbed Paul's arm to steady him, afraid that he would entirely lose control.

"No," he struggled and screamed, "I'm going to kill that monster."

Andersen escorted him back to the house to call the police. She walked back out to the yard by herself, so he wouldn't see her unraveling the line wrapped around Claudia's neck as she removed the body from the clothesline and covered it with a tarp. They waited for the police and an FBI backup to show and check for fingerprints and search more thoroughly for anything that they might've missed. The police arrived within ten minutes, and she asked them to wait for the FBI to come before they checked the place and examined the body.

Getting to Raj's office at the hospital before the killer got there was her immediate goal. Paul revealed how they'd get into the office as he pulled a key chain out of his pocket with Raj's office key attached to it. They ran the few blocks to the hospital, and as they approached, he warned that if they were seen anywhere inside the hospital especially the pathology lab, Stern or Stark would find out and stop them. As he finished saying it, the evening lab clerk walked towards them.

"Hi Doctor Peres, are you looking for some lab results?" she asked. "I'll be back in a few minutes to help you," she explained as she walked to the restroom.

"Oh shit," Paul thought. "What if she calls Stern?" He began to panic about Stern finding them and how he would explain their presence there.

No time to worry interjected Karen as though she had read his mind. Unlocking the door to Raj's office, they entered and then locked it from the inside before beginning to rummage through the room. He went through the desk as she searched the file cabinets. It seemed to be a few minutes later, that the rattling of the doorknob turning frantically drew their attention. Not answering, they froze.

A man's booming voice yelled out, "Paul, I know you're in there, open the G-D door!"

He opened it, and Stern, a short, rotund man with an enormous pot belly breathing heavily while spraying spittle from his mouth, screamed, "What the hell are you doing in my lab?"

Foolishly Paul answered, "We're looking for some of Raj's belongings that his wife said he had forgotten to bring home the night he died."

Stern exploded, "Don't F---ing lie to me, you pissant. I'll report you for breaking and entering!"

Paul sheepishly told him that Raj had given him the office key to use as needed. Stern's face twisted with fury, and he turned to Karen to ask her to show him the search warrant.

Karen erupted, "With two of your former employees' dead and one of their spouse's murdered, you're asking for a search warrant? This is an active crime scene in a murder case, and now you've become a person of interest. If you continue interfering, you'll be a suspect."

Stern backed off but stammered that they had to notify him before searching the office and lectured them on a lack of respect for his position in the hospital. Karen interrupted him and informed him that they had to get there before the killer and had no time for political correctness. Paul was unable to control his temper at that point and furiously laced into him telling him that he had no respect for him or his position. Boiling over with rage, he cursed Stern for treating Raj like shit.

Stern with a cruel smirk appeared unfazed and told them that he treated Raj as if he were part of his family and even tolerated Elaine, the slut he was first married to.

"Do you think anyone else would have given him a job in this community? He was a Muslim, who had just arrived in the country, and I hired him. He was grateful knowing that I didn't hold his religion or country of origin against him." Stern answered.

As Karen tried to defuse the squabbling, Paul became more inflamed telling him, "I'm glad I'm not in your family. You worked Raj like a slave with no recognition and a minimum salary for all the work he did for you and this poor excuse for a hospital."

Stern claimed he paid him as much as any other assistant pathologist in New York.

Paul fired back, "He did your work as well as his while you were kissing the administration's butt to establish a secure position at the medical school. I know the way you operated you bastard."

Stern responded, "I did what I had to do to protect both our positions."

Finally, she broke up the spat by warning Stern that he had to leave since they were on official FBI business. According to hospital policy, the chief claimed he had to stay there with them while they did whatever they had to do.

"That's not possible, she said. "I'm cordoning off this room and you, or anyone else entering it without permission, will end in jail."

As he was leaving, Stern warned that her superiors and hospital administration would hear about it.

She and Paul spent another hour going through the files and desk. Paul found loose slips of paper in a desk drawer with numbers scribbled on them that looked like telephone numbers. Karen recognized one with a European country code. She picked up the phone and dialed it, but the hospital operator intercepted and couldn't put an international call through without a hospital administrator's approval. Frustrated, she asked Paul where she could make the call, and he suggested they try Stark's office where she could get a direct outside line. They ran up the stairwell to the office that Paul had a key for and unlocked it.

The call went through, and the phone rang for quite a while before a man with a gruff voice answered, "Hola."

Karen hung up immediately and with a big grin said, "We've got him!"

Paul with his face pinched in puzzlement questioned why she had hung up. Explaining that it was five AM in Europe, she didn't want to tip off or anger a potential witness at that hour. Suspecting that the call went through to Spain, she surmised either the brother or someone who knew him had answered the phone.

Karen told Paul she had no doubt that the innocent twin had escaped to Spain after he had flown to France on military business. Paul questioned how she knew that.

On the way to his apartment, she elaborated that she had been to Germany to look at Reisbach's brother's military records and affirmed that the German military under Nazi rule maintained meticulous records. The government allowed foreign authorities to inspect their war documents from that era out of the fear of being accused of hiding information on those charged with war crimes. He didn't understand why she referred to Reisbach's twin as the innocent one when he too, like his brother, was probably a Nazi. Karen said he was a young cadet flight officer in the Luftwaffe which was the lowest rank in the German Air Force and it allowed him to fly an airplane on non-combat missions. He was ordered to travel to Vichy, France to deliver secret documents to the Petain government but never arrived there. Vichy wasn't under the direct military control of the Germans but had collaborated with the Nazis during the war. The story was that the brother's flight encountered an unexpected, severe storm, and the plane was believed to have crashed in the Pyrenees. Blamed on the weather and inexperience of a young pilot, the secret Nazi documents he carried were never delivered to the Vichy government. The Nazi command was enraged by the incident and began an intense search for the plane and pilot, but neither was ever found.

The missing documents resulted in a major turning point in the war since they warned of an impending Allied Forces invasion of North Africa across from France's coast. In Germany, sophisticated spying equipment had decoded the plans of the Allied Forces, but there were no rapid means of secretly conveying them to France other than by airplane delivery. They used the young, inexperienced cadet pilot as a messenger because the older experienced pilots were battling the British Royal Air Force and couldn't be spared for non-combat missions. The message never arrived there in time for the French to prepare for a naval attack from North Africa and it created the unique advantage for the Allied Forces to destroy the Axis warships in the Mediterranean Sea. Hitler had depended on the fleet to guard the southern border of Europe against the Allies and block the southern invasion of Europe from the Mediterranean.

There were theories and rumors that the airman brother had defected to the Allies with the secret papers. The Gestapo searched for him in France for years and were unsuccessful. Other theories that were proposed had him surviving after crashing in the Pyrenees but never fully confirmed, they were not pursued. The assertion was that he didn't have enough fuel for the airplane to make it across the mountains into Spain and with the freezing weather, he could never have survived crossing on foot or on the ground by any other means. The likelihood was that he never made it to Spain, and the search was concentrated in France although he was wanted throughout Europe. The war escalated and the interest to find him waned and he was presumed dead.

After the war, rumors circulated that he had survived, but it wasn't known whether he remained in Europe or fled to South America. Her brief telephone call made her suspect that Raj had been on to something that was getting too risky for Reisbach to ignore and he had to be killed. Paul thought that the importance she gave to the Spanish guy who had answered the phone was exaggerated. As tired as he was, he believed that it was a stretch to imagine that someone answering a phone in Spain meant that the brother was there. Even if he was there, he could be dead, and they'd have to find his body. Standing her ground, she couldn't be dissuaded. Shaking his head in disbelief, the realization came to him that he had joined her on her second wild goose chase for the Reisbach twin.

Chapter Seven

He received the document from the FBI declaring his father's rapidly failing health. He didn't care to examine the letter or the revised medical records describing the degree to which his dad's body was ravaged by a fatal disease. To read a sad tale even though fictional about his father's impending demise in depressing detail would have pushed him over the edge, and he handled it the only way he could by ignoring it. Preparing for the trip to Puerto Rico had created sufficient tension and the additional trauma of reading the report would only guarantee that he'd quit Andersen's scheme.

Despite Stark's outcry about personnel absences, the hospital granted a maximum of six weeks of leave. The leave was no longer a problem, but Paul's uncertainty about Karen's story of Reisbach's involvement in the Holocaust, the murders of Claudia, Elaine, Raj and all the others continued. He couldn't fully comprehend how anyone of the surgeon's advanced age was physically capable of the brutal murders without accomplices. If other killers had helped him, why didn't the police or FBI search for them? He wondered whether Stark or Stern or both could be involved and why their possible roles were not being scrutinized before he and Karen ran off to Europe? With his confidence being eroded by the minute, he began to feel weak and sweaty. His mindset was interrupted by a knock at the door and mustering the strength to respond to it, his hand trembled as he gradually unlocked the door.

Karen finished opening it and startled by his perspired grey facial complexion, she remarked, "You look like crap. What's the matter?"

Ashamed of his reaction, he tried to conceal that he had panicked again and mumbled, "It's a hypoglycemic attack from overeating sugar this morning."

"Are you diabetic?" She asked, worried that it would interfere with her plans.

"No, no," he replied, "I can't tolerate sweets or starches in the morning."

Aware that his problem was more likely cold feet rather than low blood sugar, she tried to bring him to his senses and motivate him. The telephone number found in Raj's office begged a possible Spanish connection, and the FBI traced it to Barcelona, Spain. That piece of paper that he found, she emphasized, meant that Raj and his wife knew that unraveling Reisbach's prior history would reveal the truth about him and that's why they were killed. Karen admitted that the murders were not committed by Reisbach himself but by a hired assassin. So far the pieces of the puzzle were falling into place, and she was confident that they were on the right track. He became more relaxed but continued to have trouble connecting all of it to what was found on a scrap of paper. He thought that she wasn't telling him everything she knew. She reiterated the account from Gestapo files about the evil brother hoping it would bring him to his senses. The evil brother was Joseph Mengele's assistant at Auschwitz, and as the Russian army was closing in on the concentration camp, they escaped to Spain and eventually South America. In the German war archives, the good brother on a mission to fly from Berlin to Vichy, France, was not the Reisbach, the surgeon and murderer they knew.

She waited a while before showing him two airline tickets for a flight leaving for Puerto Rico the following morning. He suddenly thought of something that might delay the whole plan. How could he go to Europe if he didn't have a passport? She reached into her pocket pulling out a shiny new one for him.

He couldn't believe it. "How did you work that?" he exclaimed!

She boasted that the agency was capable of providing documents at a moment's notice. Paul couldn't believe what he had gotten himself into. Trapped in a spider's web, no matter how hard he tried, he found himself more entangled in it.

The next day, on the plane trip he revealed that he had never flown before, no less on a four to five-hour flight from

New York to Puerto Rico. She couldn't believe that she had chosen a professional man who had never boarded an airplane and hoped it wasn't going to present another problem. After boarding, while agonizing about the explanation for the trip to his parents that Karen had arranged, he asked her what he should tell them about her presence on the journey.

Losing her patience with him, she snapped, "I told you a few days ago that we were researching a biography on Reisbach and I'm your secretary."

Shaking his head in response, he said, "I don't think they'll buy it."

"Why not?" she fumed.

"Do you think they'd believe I'm taking a leave from the hospital to write a biography and who should I say was paying for all this?" he asked.

He declared that his parents knew he never had any interest in writing. In fact, he dreaded it in college.

"Well, things change, and after all, you aren't writing it, you're just researching it," she exploded.

"There was no other doctor fluent in Spanish at the hospital that I could trust as much as you," she said tightly clenching her teeth and jaw in frustration.

He took her comment as a compliment and his temperament improved; however, Karen remained visibly annoyed and demanded that he stop acting like a child. With a set of earphones and the volume on her iPod turned up, she drowned him out and hoped it would turn him off for the rest of the trip.

Arriving at the airport in San Juan, his parents were waiting at the terminal to greet him. Karen had arranged for a ride to take her to the hotel where she had reserved a room, but he wasn't able to discourage his parents from welcoming him there. After they hugged and kissed him, his folks inspected the tall, curvaceous blonde next to him. When he had called his mother about visiting them, he never mentioned traveling with anyone. Karen quietly introduced herself as Paul's secretary accompanying him on a special project. They were surprised and not entirely satisfied by her answer. They got the luggage and left for his parent's home even though Karen said she had reserved hotel accommodations in San Juan. His parents wouldn't hear of it and insisted they go to their home.

After a short ride, they arrived at a small wood-frame cottage with a nicely manicured garden in the front yard. Pastries were set on the kitchen table, and the enticing aroma of freshly brewed coffee greeted them. After coffee and questions about the trip, his mother took his father aside wanting to know how they should plan the sleeping arrangements for their son and the unexpected female visitor in a house with only two bedrooms. They presented the problem to Paul and Karen, and she reminded them that she had the reservation in San Juan and would stay at the hotel. Although they insisted that she stay with them, she graciously wiggled her way out of it by declaring that she didn't want to interfere with Paul's visit. After coffee and small talk, although she insisted on taking a taxi, they drove to San Juan and dropped her off at the Hilton.

On the ride back to their home, they wanted to know why he hadn't said anything about the woman and the mysterious project that was planned. A barrage of questions followed while in the car. Is she really your secretary? How can you travel accompanied by a woman if you're not divorced yet? She's not Puerto Rican, is she? He managed to handle the inquisition about Karen reasonably well but explaining that he was leaving to fly to Spain the next day distressed them and didn't go well. They refused to accept it, so he revealed that he and Karen were going to interview the family of a famous New York doctor who was born and raised there.

"If the trip is only to look into the life of a colleague from Spain, it won't change that much if you stayed here with us a few days longer?" his mother insisted.

He explained that spending more time with them was out of the question since the money for the project was limited, and Karen had to get back to her regular job at the hospital. On his return home, he told them he would have more time to spend with them. They were suspicious about his relationship with the beautiful secretary, and he couldn't convince them that with her, it was all work and no play. They didn't understand what was so remarkable about a famous New York physician that a doctor and secretary were needed when a Spanish speaking secretary alone could handle it. He tried to manage the bombardment of questions with as many rational answers that he could summon.

He swore them to secrecy about the plan with the female traveling companion, warning them that with the pending divorce, no one including Maria should be told about his trip or plan. They were taken aback by his request and didn't understand the need for secrecy. It was a stretch for him to find an answer that would satisfy them but he shocked them with the information that Maria had taken him to court to take the children away from him. They weren't aware of the court battle over the children and to protect him, agreed not to say anything to her or anyone else. Reassured, he passed the remainder of the evening asking about their activities, health, and finances but felt guilty that he had dragged them into his quagmire.

Up early the next morning, they insisted on driving him to the airport. He convinced them a taxi would be better since the international terminal might be too difficult to find and Karen would be waiting there to meet him. Meeting up with Karen at the airport, he discovered that they were flying back on an FBI jet to Miami. Surprised, he wanted to know why?

"You had to see your parents and take care of your father," she answered.

He replied, "Don't bullshit me. What's the real reason?"

"I could only get a direct flight to Barcelona from Miami," she stated.

She wouldn't risk telling him that the real reason for using the agency jet to Miami was to prevent his name from showing up on an airline's manifest list of passengers that would reveal that he had departed from the island to fly to Europe. Appearing that he never left Puerto Rico was consistent with the family leave story and would throw Reisbach off their trail if they were being followed. Her immediate plan also included not telling him that he was traveling with a phony passport concealing his identity so that no one would know he had flown to Spain and track them down. She had to tell him that he had a fake passport but decided to wait, and tell him when they were ready to clear customs at the airport in Spain. It would spare her from the multitude of questions that she expected he would ask on the flight to Europe.

Chapter Eight

---◆◆◆---

M iami International airport rivals New York's JFK Airport for its congestion and confusion more than any other airport in the world. The only difference was with Miami's more massive Hispanic influence knowing a little bit of Spanish goes a long way in greasing the wheels of the airport to navigate through it more efficiently. Paul's modest grasp of the language smoothed their way through the airport but didn't soothe Karen's anxiety about sitting next to him in coach for several more hours. With the fear that he would grill her with questions demanding her constant attention, she wondered how she would keep him busy. She was relieved, he had taken medical journals with him to read during the flight and hoped it would keep him distracted from asking about the details of the Barcelona trip. To divert his questions, she began asking him about his wife and the reason for the divorce. She whispered if another man or woman had caused it? With an abrupt no, he began to tell her.

Seemingly amused by her question, he chuckled that it wasn't anything as ordinary as that. His wife didn't want to leave the South Bronx and live in northern Westchester when he gave up his private practice in the Bronx and accepted the position at the hospital in Westchester. Maria's issue wasn't about leaving the practice behind but deserting her adoring friends and family in the Bronx. Moving to the suburbs and adjusting to life in unfamiliar surroundings that she hadn't grown up in terrified her as if kidnaped to a foreign country. She ridiculed suburban life protesting that she had nothing in common with the women in Westchester and didn't want to raise children spoiled by those values. Although Maria wasn't born or raised in Puerto Rico, her parents were from the old school and instilled in her the customs of the old country. Joking, he said they lived in the South Bronx that was unofficially known as Puerto Rico del Norte. Paul hated where they lived and the lifestyle and found practicing medicine there unrewarding. Commuting back and forth to work from there would have been impossible with the demands of the new job that he had accepted at North County Hospital. They rented a house in Westchester for a couple of years while he worked there. She was unhappy, and after years of arguing and counseling, they agreed that they had irreconcilable differences.

Karen's eyelids widened in surprise, and she couldn't understand how anyone would object to leaving the Bronx. Her impression was that they had similar backgrounds and the marriage would have been stronger. The difference he explained was that his parents expected him to adopt North American standards. Prying further, she asked him how he and his wife were attracted to each other if their upbringing was that different.

He reminded Karen that they had attended the same schools, and said he wanted her, the most beautiful girl in the high school, for his wife. Their families although differing in cultural values seemed pleased with their courtship. His mother thought his future wife's old-world upbringing and lack of extravagant tastes made her solid marriage material and Maria's parents couldn't think of anyone better than a doctor to have as a son-in-law. They married while he was in medical school. After the wedding, she worked as a secretary, and they lived with his family.

After they moved to Westchester, Maria blamed him for being a lousy husband who had disrupted her life. After leaving him and returning to the Bronx with the kids, she denounced him as a neglectful husband and father for not devoting enough time with the kids and separating her from her family and friends. He could never get her to appreciate that practicing medicine was a twenty-four hour and seven day a week profession that interfered with a normal family life. As a last straw, she demanded sole custody of the children. That's terrible Karen responded and sensed it was a painful topic for him to continue to discuss, so she steered away from any further conversation of his wife and kids.

She encouraged him to talk about his childhood. He explained that it was a challenge attending a parochial school in the Bronx because he walked to school and the neighborhood and public-school kids always harassed and bullied him about the required Catholic school uniform that he wore consisting of a long sleeve white shirt, tie, and long pants. Frequently beaten up by gang members because of his clothes or just because they didn't like his looks, he'd walk different routes to and from school. If that didn't work, to leave him alone, he'd bribe them with his allowance money for lunch, so he wouldn't go home all bloodied. As he got older, the drug scene was happening all around him and getting mugged at knife or gunpoint was not unusual. Despite the drugs and crime in the neighborhood, he did well in school. His mother was overly protective and didn't want him outside playing sports after school because of all the random shootings from gang fights. It wasn't unusual to hear gunfire day and night in abandoned apartment buildings and staying out after dark meant taking one's life in their hands. The cops at the time called the neighborhood Fort Apache. He said he really didn't like living there as a child and even though the neighborhood had improved with time, picturing himself living there as an adult was demoralizing. He couldn't wait to leave and live anywhere else. Wow, she thought what she had missed out on growing up in Idaho. The tone of the conversation about his childhood had become depressing and saddening her, she was eager to change the subject.

She wanted him to recount how he became friends with Raj and what their relationship was like. That seemed to relax him, and he explained that they both hit it off from the beginning. Other than the practice of medicine, they had nothing in common with the other staff physicians. Raj was admired because he was smarter and more sophisticated than most of the doctors he had met in his medical career. He was knowledgeable about medicine, the world, and culture.

With a special interest in politics and European history, he enjoyed reading the British and European newspapers and discussing world affairs and life including the culture during the nineteen sixties and seventies in the United States. Raj regretted missing all the excitement of the period by living in Iran and not being in the States at that time, but he knew more about that era than anyone growing up in New York. Even though he envied Raj's worldliness and realized he'd never enjoy the same experiences, Paul admitted that he was happy they shared a special bond despite their different ethnic backgrounds. Culturally different from other physicians on the staff, they were the outsiders in the cosmos of their hospital. Continuing about his friend's relationship with his boss Stern and ex-wife Elaine, he described her as beautiful, young and full of life which was what Raj adored about her. She had been studying for her doctorate in pharmacology and Raj was able to help her with his incredible knowledge of pathology. With her studies and job, and Raj's overloaded work schedule, they seldom had time to be with one another. At bedtime, they were too tired for anything but sleep which created the highest tension in their marriage. Stern had recommended her for the position in Reisbach's research lab since she could no longer work for him because Raj was in the same department.

Working with Reisbach's research group as a pharmacology assistant pleased Elaine but bothered Raj. He felt obligated to his boss for getting her the job, and Stern took advantage of that by piling on more work for him. She was enthusiastic about her new role and tried to learn every aspect of transplantation medicine. While attempting to produce a less toxic anti-rejection drug for use in human trials, she discussed her work with Raj who recognized that Stark, as the head of the research committee thwarted her progress. Reisbach and Stark wanted the drug approved despite its toxic side effects, and she was alarmed by the number of patients who received it and had severe reactions that were not being reported to the FDA. Even though she expressed her concerns at the research meetings, the members of the committee didn't appreciate the problem and would side with Stark who either ignored or downplayed her findings and completely frustrated her efforts. Paul emphasized that Reisbach, the administration and some of the full-time senior staff had vested interests in having the drug approved and didn't hinder Stark's attack of her work. They knew the hospital's fate depended on the drug's approval and once cleared by the FDA, big pharma would pay millions for the rights to produce and sell it.

The future of the hospital was at stake, and its solvency could not depend solely on a takeover by a medical school. There was a lot riding on the drug and Reisbach, Stark, and Stern had invested their careers and wealth trying to get the drug into the marketplace. Elaine knew what she was up against and had planned to go directly to the FDA with her concerns but that wouldn't happen with her dead. Reflecting on it Paul said maybe the cops, Stern and Stark were right, the murder, after all was drug-related.

All of this seemed too familiar to Karen whose father had been a pharmacist working for Reisbach in Idaho and it was thought that he had similar concerns then about the surgeon and his research. As a result, she believed her father was eliminated, however at the time, she was too young to understand what the problem was or its connection to his death. In the community in Idaho, there were many rumors about Reisbach including one that was spread about supporting neo-Nazi organizations with the money made from his research. Karen uncomfortable talking about the circumstances surrounding her father's murder switched the narrative to the college town that she had grown up in.

German immigrants had initially settled in Northern Idaho before World War Two. Her parents, however, emigrated from Germany after the War. Her father in Germany had taught chemistry at Bonn University, and her mother was a typical German hausfrau. Her mother had a thick accent that most Americans could not decipher. Her father, who was an educated man, spoke perfect English. Growing up as an only child, her father doted over her and she was closer to him than her mother. Her mother was a cold and distant person disappointed that she had not given birth to a son and wasn't affectionate towards her daughter. The mother seemed to favor men more than women and her father was not one of the most esteemed men in her mother's life. Her parents frequently argued about his defiant attitude towards the man he worked for. His wife worshiped Reisbach and thought of him as a god who had rescued them from the fall of Germany by using his clout to sponsor their immigration to the USA. Her mother always claimed that Germans were not welcomed in the States after the war and could not understand her husband's attitude towards someone they were beholden to. Despite her mother's belief, Karen's father had received special consideration to emigrate because he was a scientist and didn't need Reisbach's sponsorship. Karen told Paul she couldn't wait to leave home and go away to college where she majored in political science. A big hit with the college guys, she could drink more beer than most of them. Her grades were excellent and passed the required acceptance exams for the FBI. Enjoying the FBI milieu, she bragged that working with good-looking guys who flirted with her wasn't all that bad. Claiming to be a good sport about the sex-laced comments she received from men at the agency, political correctness never interfered with her replying to them with similar provocations. For her first assignment, she was given the task of investigating the suspicious deaths that had taken place in her hometown which remained unsolved. Deeply troubled by them since her youth, she energetically dug into investigating them at the time.

She had returned home when her mother was dying of cancer and had only Karen to attend to her. Caring for someone who had never shown her any love was a bitter reality that threw her into a deep depression. Her mother's personality hadn't changed, and she remained cold and detached even as she was dying. There was no remorse shown for the lack of affection she had displayed towards her daughter. Karen admitted it was the darkest period of her life and after her mother died she began drinking at the local bars in town where she met her future alcoholic husband. Her friends from high school and college had moved on and no longer worked or lived in the community. Feeling abandoned and for all the wrong reasons, she married. The marriage didn't last a year and ended in divorce. Since her maiden name was a German tongue-twister, she adopted her ex-husband's name.

They talked during most of the flight and eventually fell asleep. The flight landed on time and arrived late that evening. A car provided by the FBI was waiting for them at the airport and drove to a nondescript hotel that looked like any dismal apartment house built during the nineteen fifties in an unfashionable neighborhood of New York City. Above the entrance door that opened to the lobby hung a small almost illegible sign indicating it was a hotel. They awakened the doorman in the small lobby who doubled as the desk clerk. Coming out of a deep sleep, he ran behind a counter to greet them and sign them in. The only attractive feature of the hotel that they would appreciate in the morning was its location on a side street off Las Ramblas, the famous boulevard traversing Barcelona with easy access to the local shops and restaurants.

The adjoining rooms reserved for them were the typical European size that was considered small by American criteria. The decor was slightly more pleasant than a mid-western YMCA or cheap motel in the States. It was not in the grand style of Antoni Gaudi, the world-famous Barcelona architect, and artist whose architectural wonders the city was noted for, but it was clean and tidy. Following a long flight, they were too beat to notice or protest, and with early plans for the following day, retired to their rooms.

Chapter Nine

Despite the long flight, they were up at sunrise and had breakfast in the hotel. Breakfast was the typical continental fare, but Paul had wanted eggs and bacon. He asked Karen where he could get a hot meal, but she told him European hotels served continental breakfasts and not to complain. If he wanted an American one, they would have had to stay in an American hotel, and that wasn't going to happen according to Karen.

She then said, "The Spanish authorities and Interpol have checked out the phone number you found and can't trace it to an individual or business."

It was from a cellphone that was apparently paid for with cash and used prepaid phone cards that didn't require identification. The same type of phone that drug dealers and terrorists use to elude the police and FBI.

Paul sat there in disbelief. "Then what are we doing here in Barcelona?" he snapped at her.

Karen said that Barcelona was the area the number originated from when it was checked by the phone company, and it was a start.

Disgusted he asked, "What if the phone was bought in Barcelona and he answered the call in Italy?"

She ignored him and pointedly said that they were going to the Barcelona census bureau to find any current or past records listing a Reisbach and maybe they'll find his brother or other family members that way. She had received clearance to use the office on Via Laietana, which wasn't far from the hotel.

"What happens if we don't find his name or a similar name in the census records? Do we fly home?" he argued.

Trying to remain calm, she quietly stated there were other ways to find someone and decided to have a leisurely breakfast. Paul was eager to find a Starbucks or any other American fast-food restaurant. Waiting until mid-morning to go to the bureau, she believed they would be more likely to find a manager to talk to rather than hassling with a department clerk. As a foreigner, she had to produce identification and documentation permitting her to review their files. It was rumored that Spanish bureaucrats didn't start their work day before ten AM because they generally had their last meal of the day at ten or eleven PM. Paul looked at a tourist map to find the location of the census department on Via Laietana. He pointed out that they were only a few blocks away and could walk there while taking in the sites of the Gaudi district of the city.

She chimed in and said, "We're not walking around while in Barcelona. Anywhere we go we take a cab or rent a car to get there."

With a puzzled look on his face he asked, "Why?"

With a piercing stare, she said, "Strolling the boulevards and peering into shop windows is the easiest way an assassin can find us. Anywhere we go, we travel by a rental car or taxi and avoid public transportation."

During the extra time they had following breakfast, he had read about the unusual futuristic designs of Gaudi and wasn't happy about what she had said. Although the hotel was not constructed to Gaudi's architectural specifications, it was in the heart of the Gaudi district of the city and surrounded by the amazingly ornate designs and gaudy artwork that the Spanish architect had created during his lifetime. Paul was interested in exploring the area. After some discussion, they decided to meet in the lobby after freshening up in their rooms. A taxi brought them directly to the census bureau and Paul didn't see much of the architecture of Gaudi on the way.

After waiting patiently to see the director, they were pleasantly surprised by his Spanish charm and unusually cooperative manner. He spoke excellent English, so there was no need for Paul to translate. Karen, however, hadn't planned on all the registration documents written in Spanish, and Paul had to interpret them. The information was computerized and Reisbach's name didn't appear in the unending lists of names and addresses. Paul had suspected as much and was about to say something sarcastic when she told him, they were going to plan B. Having no idea what that was, she explained they would look for surnames with a similar spelling.

The process proved tedious and Paul going bonkers with a sudden outburst raising his voice said, "What the hell are we doing here? You could have had one of the bureau clerks do this job for you instead of wasting all this time."

Remaining unusually calm, she told him she hadn't wanted anyone to know who they were looking for and told him to release some steam and take a long walk in the building. He agreed since he had to find a restroom. Karen double checked every name and address that he had listed to make sure that he included all similar German surnames. There were thousands of Germans living in Barcelona and the surrounding regions according to the most recent census. Spain had always been an ideal place for the Germans to vacation. Many flocked to the beaches of southern Spain, and some never left. Paul asked her what she was going to do with all the names and addresses of the people they had retrieved.

"You realize his name hasn't appeared in the census," he quipped.

He suggested a search of death certificates, but she said she had done that on her computer at the FBI agency. She hadn't found his name listed that way either. Totally exasperated and in a huff, he started his search for a toilet. He couldn't locate the men's restroom, so he returned and asked the cute file room clerk where to look for one. Attractive and very friendly, her wide beautiful brown eyes were captivating, and he remembered a song his mother sang called "Spanish Eyes." He had never seen eyes like those in the Puerto Rican girls he had dated at home. Now he knew what had inspired the title of the song and it fascinated him, as he heard it in his head as though his mother was singing it.

The young clerk asked what he was doing at the census bureau and where he was from in the States. After telling him that her dream was to travel to the United States, especially New York City, she asked who they were looking for in Barcelona. Her eyes grew even wider as he replied that he was from New York, and they were trying to find the brother of a famous person in New York. To quell her curiosity about who they were hoping to find, he insisted that he couldn't reveal his name, but said his family originated in Germany and his brother lived in Barcelona.

Suspicious about the secretive way he answered, her eyelids retracted pensively as she thought a while before looking at him to tell him about a German community center on Carrer Brise. She said the street wasn't far from the bureau and the people there might be able to help. Smiling sweetly, she told him there was an elderly lady in the center who had lived in the city for years and knew most of the prominent German families who now live or ever lived in Barcelona. Continuing to voice her interest in New York, she told him she'd love to hear about New York if he had the opportunity to tell her about the city. Excited about giving Karen the information about the community center, he said he didn't have time to spare at that moment but later in the day might be a better time for him to discuss it with her. After asking if she was available after work, she handed Paul a note with her name and telephone number and he promised to call.

With a swagger, he returned to the office where Karen remained. Feeling a lot better about Barcelona and the visit to the bureau, he demanded that Karen stop wasting her time. She didn't like his tone of voice and told him not to harass her.

He proudly boasted, "I've found the best way to find a German in this town."

She tried to ignore him and said, "I'll bet."

He retorted, "Seriously."

He told her he had a lead on how to find the brother if he was anywhere in Barcelona. She listened to what he had to say and decided to find the community center. On the way, they stopped for a quick lunch since it was already noon. He teased her that asking the locals was a better idea than searching the census files. She wasn't happy how he found out about the new source and worried that it was dangerous if the gal who gave him the information started talking about two Americans looking for a German in Barcelona. In any event, Paul still believed that even with the new information, they had a slim chance of finding Reisbach's twin brother.

Following lunch, they hailed a taxi to take them to the center on Carrer Brise. They rode northwest on Via Laietana until they got to Placa d'Antoni Maura and encountering heavy traffic, the driver zigzagged in and out of crossing streets that were difficult to remember or follow without a GPS or map. She was wary about where they were being taken and whether they would find their way back to the hotel on their own. The driver stopped across the street from a stone chapel and pointed to a building across from an enclosed parking lot. Paul paid the fare as he asked if it was the center and couldn't understand the driver's directions in the strange Catalan language that some of the Barcelonans spoke.

They were directed to a white stucco building adjacent to a tiny park across the street. They walked past the parking lot to a building and asked someone who was leaving if it was the center. Told to continue to walk through the park, they saw a white stucco building with a sign identifying it as a gift shop. Assuming it was the entrance to the center, they entered a small room with a young lady seated reading a magazine surrounded by shelves and racks cluttered with souvenirs, books and magazines, many of them in the German language. With the realization that they were in the right place, he politely confirmed where they were with the gal reading the magazine and asked if there was a woman there who could help them find someone in Barcelona. She replied that the old lady who owned the shop knew every German that ever resided in Barcelona. The remark raised a smile on both their faces and they simultaneously asked if she was there. The attendant told them that the senora only came in late in the day at about five or six PM to check the receipts from the gift shop and to lock up. Disappointed, they wondered what they were going to do in the interim as they waited. They thanked the gal and walked out to sit on a park bench to plan their next move. Karen was prepared to hear Paul boast and not let her forget that he had found the new source. He, however, seemed preoccupied and surprised her by not mentioning the center. They had time to see some of the sights, and he wanted to go to Guell Park, a favorite tourist attraction designed by Antoni Gaudi.

The pitch of his voice rose gently to a higher level like a child eagerly trying to persuade his mother to take him somewhere, and the words tumbled out, "There are buildings and gardens there like no other on earth. It can't be that far away!"

With a curt response, she answered, "It's not going to happen."

She claimed that she had been there and knew it was a perfect place for a surprise attack by anyone out to kill them. She remembered it as an Alice in Wonderland park with all sorts of distorted structures as though it was designed on drugs. A tail following them would have the perfect opportunity to kill them, she warned. With the strangely designed meandering walkways, lopsided buildings and crazily patterned stonework, it was the ideal place for an assassin to get away with murder. Realizing he probably read about the park in one of the tourist pamphlets in the hotel, she wasn't about to please him and walk into a setting that was dangerous for them and any innocent bystanders.

He angrily replied, "We are easier targets sitting on a bench in a sun-filled park at midday with mothers pushing children in strollers than walking through a maze of walkways and buildings."

She realized that he was like a kid who had only seen the world from pictures in books, and against her better judgement decided to take him there. They asked for directions to Guell Park from the girl in the shop and left Carrer Brise about two PM. Karen warned him not to wander, and to stay tightly to her side. She walked with one hand on the semi-automatic handgun tucked in her waistband while showing him the attractions in the park. At the entrance to the park, a giant statue of a dragon covered with thousands of multicolored mosaic tiles shining in the sunlight greeted them. Karen refused to take a photo of him standing next to it. The view of Barcelona from the highest point in the park was truly spectacular, and they could see all the way to the bay and Mediterranean Sea. Without encountering any danger in the park, they returned to the community center just before five PM.

They walked to the white stucco building and found the door locked. Unable to open it, they knocked loudly several times, and louder with each attempt. Finally, the door slowly opened, and an elderly woman peeked out asking who they were. Paul explained in halting Spanish that they had been there earlier and needed her help to find someone in Barcelona. Yes, the woman replied, Regina, my assistant, told me about you before she left for the day. They entered and got a better look at the stooped lady with the bright blue-white hair, whose ancient visage indicated that her age exceeded the lifespan of any living person they had ever seen before. Paul guessed that she was at least one hundred years old, but her speech defied her age and was not weak or muffled as expected by her biblical appearance. She only spoke Spanish, and Karen had to rely on Paul to translate. Asking them to provide identification, he showed her his hospital identification badge with a photo of him in a white lab coat. She asked them what they wished to know, and he explained he was writing a biography and looking for a relative of the person he was writing about. She asked who the person was that he was writing about. He explained it was a famous New York doctor, who had lost contact with his family after the last World War and believed his brother now lived in Barcelona but hadn't been able locate him. She questioned why the doctor required their help to find the brother and wasn't searching on his own. Paul related that the man he spoke of was too old to travel. She nodded her head and in the local Catalan dialect, replied "com jo." When they mentioned the name of the individual, her gaze froze with an ice-cold presence that changed her softly furrowed face to stone and with the unmistakable silence of apprehension, it seemed as if she would never reply. She told them she didn't know whether he was dead or alive and had not lived in Barcelona for quite some time, further emphasizing that she didn't know where he was. Paul with prompting from Karen asked if she knew anything that she could tell them about him.

She abruptly answered, "No."

They sensed she wasn't going to give them more information, but Paul gently clasped her withered hand in his hands and softly in his best Spanish asked if there were any friends or relatives living in the city, who might know what happened to him. She hesitated and gently said he had a daughter. After more coaxing, she admitted that she didn't know her married name, but the daughter had owned a dress shop on Ramblas Boulevard near the Rivoli hotel. They refrained from asking more question feeling that all the air in the room had been used up, and no further discussion would follow. It was the signal that it was time for them to leave the delicate old lady to her memories without intruding further. Karen gracefully said muchas gracias and held the old lady's gnarled hand in gratitude. Paul added some kind words in Spanish and they left.

It was about six PM, and they were both excited about the information. They walked briskly through the park to hail a taxi. Karen wondered if they'd find the daughter's store open that evening. Many of the shops closed for siesta in the afternoon and reopened again at night until ten PM. The traffic was heavy, and when they got to the store it was dark and the door was locked. Paul looked for the store hours posted on the door and saw that it wasn't reopening that night. He returned to the taxi and informed Karen. They decided on a quick dinner and afterward walked back to the hotel.

After returning to his room, Paul fell asleep while watching television. The sound of laughter coming from the TV awakened him. He looked at the clock on the bed stand and saw that it was nine PM. Digging in his wallet for the slip of paper with the file clerk's telephone number, he wondered if it was too late to call. Despite the hour, he dialed the number, and she answered "Hola Clara." They talked a short while about the day's events. The girl asked if he wanted to come to her place or go out for a drink. After telling her that he didn't have a car or know his way around town well enough to take public transportation, she offered to come to the hotel. He suggested that they meet at a Starbucks just a block away from the hotel. Without any hesitation, she agreed.

He walked to the Starbucks that he had seen earlier that day. While ordering a tall cafe latte, he saw egg sandwiches with bacon on an English muffin in the glass cabinet. No more continental breakfasts for him, he decided while sipping his latte. Seated at a corner table, he saw her entering and quickly rose to offer her a drink.

"Chai," she whispered.

They got comfortable and immediately began talking. Clara asked what his opinion was of Barcelona and the places he had visited. She offered to escort him to the sites he hadn't seen but could only do it on the weekend when she was not working. The conversation drifted to the usual vital statistics including what he did for a living and to her surprise learned that he was a doctor writing a book which was why he was in Spain. Rolling her beautiful eyes in wonder, she asked what kind of a doctor he was and why he had chosen Barcelona to write his book? She continued to tell him that in his spare time he should take in all the attractions in the city, rattling off a list of the most popular sites that included a tour of La Rambla Boulevard and the Sagrada Cathedral built in the grand architectural style of Gaudi. She then wanted to know all about New York.

They spent about an hour talking while finishing their drinks and he talked about New York City and the places to visit there. After describing Central Park, the Empire State Building and the Statute of Liberty, he told her that he practiced medicine in a suburb of New York City and specialized in internal medicine. Concerning the reason for his trip to Barcelona, he conveyed the tale that Karen had created with slight variations. It was a search for the family of a famous physician colleague who he had worked with on a research project in the States. He excused the paucity of details with the apology of not wanting to bore her and thanked her for the invaluable advice about the community center. Trying to show his gratitude for help, he said he would be delighted if she could show him around town.

Apologizing that he hadn't offered her anything to eat, he suddenly froze as he sat there and saw Karen entering the café. Fortunately, Clara was sitting with her back to the entrance as Karen walked in. Paul knew that she had spotted him because her face bristled with a dark non-verbal snarl that had bolted him upright in his chair. His young guest didn't see Andersen walk in and assumed the doctor was suddenly overcome with some terrible malady. His color turned ashen grey and his strange reaction frightened her as it appeared he would collapse. Gradually recovering his demeanor and using his experience in the art of the medical excuse, he blamed his trouble on volcanic eruptions in his gut from a rich Catalan meal he had eaten that day that he wasn't accustomed to eating. He tried to keep his guest's full attention as Karen walked to the counter and ordered a coffee. After Karen paid the barista, she slowly passed by his table and delivered another unspoken message with a sneer that rang out loud and clear that he had done something that was strictly verboten! Grateful that she hadn't created a scene, he let out with a loud sigh of relief that was misconstrued by his evening companion as a near fatal attack requiring emergency medical treatment at a hospital. He explained that it was the sound of relief and he was feeling better but thought they should call it a night. Offering to pay for a cab to take her home, she declined but asked him to accompany her to the nearest Metro station.

Karen was waiting for him in the hotel lobby. He could see she was ready to boil over and pounce on him but controlling her temper she waited until they were in the elevator. She told him that his soiree with the girl was a dumb F---ing idea, and he could have endangered the girl's life. He looked puzzled and remarked it was only Starbucks and a cup of coffee. Curious to know how she found where he was, she explained that she had planted a tracking device on him. Hearing that, he began briskly moving both hands over his body searching for the device in his shirt and pants. Unsuccessful, he asked where she had hidden it.

"In your butt, where the sun doesn't shine, and your brain seems to be located," was her biting reply.

He asked, "Honestly how did you know I was there?"

She told him she tried calling him to discuss the plans for the following day and when he didn't answer, she opened the adjoining door to his room and didn't see him there. Her first thought was that he had been kidnapped. She realized the room didn't appear as though there was a struggle and with the strong scent of cologne in the room, she figured he had gone out. She had a notion that he wouldn't go too far and concluded he had gone to the nearest Starbucks. He still didn't fully grasp the significance of how he could have gotten the girl killed. She looked disappointed and in no uncertain terms said that they were probably being followed by an assassin. With her voice full of anger, she stressed that the girl could have been killed by a bullet meant for him or could have been captured and tortured until she told her captors what she knew and then murdered. As they entered their adjacent rooms, he was sullen and agreed it was a stupid move on his part. Apologizing, he told her that she was right, and he was sorry. He felt terrible about the incident, promising it wouldn't happen again.

In his room, he tried to recall what had happened that day. He reflected on his reaction to the gal in the census bureau and how she had offered him her telephone number without any hesitation or his asking for it. That sort of thing never happened to him in New York and certainly not in the Bronx. Was he so appealing that a young woman would just offer him her phone number like that or did she really want to hear about New York from a native? Were women in Spain that open that they didn't hesitate to give that sort of information to strangers before knowing who they were? He certainly never felt that freedom in the States. He wondered if all the women would be so inviting on this trip that he had initially hesitated to take. If they were that spontaneous, he would like it there. In New York, he had never had that degree of freedom and certainly not in the hospital. He remembered as a resident some of his friends got in trouble for approaching secretaries and nurses for dates. Some of them were reported to their chiefs and hospital administration for sexual harassment. You certainly couldn't put a hand on a nurse's shoulder to tell her how much you appreciated her help without fearing she'd report you as a sexual deviant and, the touchy-feely sort of guys were probably locked up in an asylum or prison somewhere. No wonder he felt suffocated back home and here felt like he was waking from the dead and not waking dead as he did every day at home.

Karen was in her room reflecting on Paul's reactions during the day. For a guy she thought was rather backward, he turned out to be rather aggressive. She worried about his unabashed ability to approach a young woman with such ease. With her earlier assessment that a great deal of his behavior was neurotic and self-conscious, she had totally missed the mark. Now she worried that he was a possible blossoming sexual predator trying to bed any pretty young thing he could coerce with his Latin charm. He hadn't impressed her as full-blown lothario by his reluctant and defiant interactions with her but it genuinely puzzled and disturbed her that his unpredictable conduct with women might create an insurmountable problem for her. What if a jealous husband or boyfriend caught him at his game? He could ruin her investigative effort and her only hope was that the incident that evening was an isolated one. However, she was aware that visitors to foreign countries often thought they were free to act without the restraint that they had at home. That also troubled her and whatever was causing his actions, she had to keep a close eye on him.

Chapter Ten

In the morning they walked to Starbucks for breakfast and to Paul's surprise, Karen ordered the English muffin with egg, cheese, and sausage. After their confrontation the night before, he didn't make any snide remarks about her choice. In fact, it was his quietest day so far on the trip, and Karen figured that after acting like a fool it was his atonement for the lapse of judgment on the prior night. He didn't think he would see the attractive young woman from the census bureau again, and that depressed him. She was wonderfully relaxed and pleasant compared to his wife or Karen. If his current circumstance weren't as threatening, he would contact her again. After coffee and an egg sandwich, he felt better while waiting to hear what Karen's plan was for the day.

The dress shop opened at ten in the morning, and he really wanted to explore the local area before heading to La Ramblas, but he dared not suggest it. At about a quarter after nine, they walked back to the hotel, and a car supplied by the FBI was waiting for them. Karen had requested the vehicle because of the difficulty finding taxis in the height of the traffic hour on the prior day. The valet went to retrieve it, and she saw that the car was parked on a lift in an open lot across from the hotel. She immediately realized that the garaging arrangement would present a problem if the vehicle were needed for a quick getaway. She tried to persuade the concierge to store it on the lowest level but was told that all the parking spots on the ground level had been taken by the long-term residential guests.

It was a short drive to the dress shop which was open, and they parked nearby. As they entered the store, Paul speaking Spanish asked the sales girl if the owner was available. He was surprised when she answered that she was the owner of the shop, Margarita Lofuego. Not expecting someone as young and attractive, his thought was that she possibly was the granddaughter rather than his daughter. After introducing himself as a physician from the USA, he told her he wished to inquire about her father. Her facial muscles tightened with a terrified look on her face, and her voice quivered as she asked why. Repeating the story that he and Karen had rehearsed about writing a biography of the uncle from New York, he said he wished to talk to her father about his brother.

She denied that her father had a brother in the United States and said, "My father is dead!"

Fearful of his objective, she asked, "Why do you want to write a book about his twin?"

She claimed that she really didn't know her father, and he had been dead for fifteen years. They asked about his past, and she adamantly refused to answer. After a long pause she added, that if he were alive, he wouldn't want to talk about his brother. Furthermore, she continued that she didn't even know where he was buried since he had abandoned his family when she was a young child and moved away a long time ago. Turning away from them, she said she couldn't help them. Paul sensed that Lofuego suspected that they were there for some reason other than questioning him and she wouldn't tell them a thing. He pressured her that they really had to find out if he was alive because it was personal information they needed to know that she might not be familiar with. With unrestrained bitterness, the lady told them to get out of her store. Her father had suffered enough, and if they didn't leave immediately, she would call the police. If he were alive, she admonished that having to relive his experience during and after the war was pain and suffering that a man his age shouldn't have to endure. Paul said he didn't understand and tried to get her to explain what she meant.

She told him her father had been a Luftwaffe pilot during World War Two who had never wanted to fight in the German army but his father physically tortured him until he enlisted. He deserted to Spain shortly after he had joined the Luftwaffe and the Nazis hunted him like an animal making his life unbearable during and after the war. To avoid detection, he continuously moved to different locations and changed his identity every time. Even when the war ended, General Franco's militia wanted him expatriated to Germany, and they continued to pursue him. After he married my mother and took her last name as his, both governments continued to harass him and her family. She could never subject him to that again. Karen, from Paul's interpretation, believed that her protest was an implicit admission that he was alive, and she knew where he was hiding. Margarita hurriedly said she had to close the shop at noon and did not wish to speak to them any longer. In a soft tone, Paul changed the tenor of the conversation and admired the shop and its merchandise with kind remarks about the decor and youthful selection of dresses and apparel that was displayed.

Apologizing for disturbing her, he explained that he was not there to stalk her father and only wished she could answer some more questions. He then asked if she would join them for lunch.

Surprising him she responded, "Si."

Karen not fully understanding what was said, asked, "What did she agree to do?"

He told her that he had explained that they weren't there to track down her father and would only record the family history that she was willing to give them.

Karen appearing doubtful asked, "Then how are we going to find him?"

He responded that he had asked Margarita to join them for lunch and thought some wine and coddling might loosen her up enough to reveal her father's location.

Margarita brought them to a local eatery, and Paul had difficulty understanding the menu since it was written in Catalan, the language used in Barcelona and Margarita ordered for them. While waiting for their food, she told him that she had never met her paternal grandfather and had heard he was a violent man who frequently beat his sons for no apparent reason even as they became adults. Her father's twin brother was just as vicious as his father. She couldn't believe he had become a doctor. Her dad, by comparison, was a gentle, compassionate man who never seemed to get along with his brother. He frequently referred to him as the monster. Turning her head to peer around the restaurant, she cautiously whispered, her uncle was responsible for many atrocities during the war.

With a delicious meal and potent local red wine, she began to mellow and opened up more readily about her family. She went on to tell them that her uncle had visited them several times during and after the war, and with each visit, her father would become depressed. Her father was never happy to see his brother and eventually refused to see him or communicate with him in any way. With time, there was a gradual change in his temperament from a doting parent, he became a recluse who avoided everyone including his wife and daughter. As a child, Margarita didn't understand why he had become so detached and begged her mother for an explanation.

Later in life, as her mother was dying, she revealed the reason for her husband's withdrawn behavior and blamed it on the horrible atrocities during the war and the uncle's role in them. She told her daughter that the uncle had been recruited as a young college student to work with Doctor Mengele and his research studying the physical traits of Jewish twins in the concentration camp. His role was to find suitable subjects for Mengele's study and maintain the records of Mengele's experiments. Because her uncle did his job so well, his duties were expanded to performing blood tests and tissue samples of the subjects and eventually assisted his mentor in the experimental surgery. Of course, she stressed, all the operations performed in Auschwitz were inhumane and without anesthesia. Before their surgery, the research subjects would be marched into the gas chamber with all the victims who were selected to die, and when they lost consciousness, Mengele had them taken out of the gas chamber and performed the operation on them. Although alive and unconscious when taken out of the chamber, most of them awakened during the operations horrified, painfully seeing their bodies mutilated. Many believed they were waking dead and being tortured in hell. Those who survived the surgery eventually died of complications from the bungled operations and terrible infections. If that didn't kill them, they lived with horribly disfigured bodies, many of them beyond recognition and with permanent physical and psychic scars.

The uncle claimed Mengele's research was pointless sadistic experimentation with no scientific purpose to justify removing internal organs from identical or fraternal twins and then compare them for variations when there were none. Mengele did the same experiments on prisoners who weren't twins and compared the results to his findings from the twins for no rational purpose or possible scientific benefit since normal human organs all appear the same.

As she explained all that, tears rolled down her face, and she cried that the prisoners were better off dying in the gas chamber and not surviving the horrible fate that awaited them when they became Mengele's experimental subjects. Even her terrible uncle didn't understand why Mengele performed the surgery and hadn't stopped when it was apparent that it was madness with no scientific value. The father's twin seemed to recognize that our bodies were all the same internally and didn't support his mentor's deranged ideas but had more sophisticated plans that were just as cruel and inhumane which he rationalized as having genuine scientific value. Learning of animal experiments in his college biology studies that proved that a limb or other body part removed from an animal and grafted it to another of the same species survived successfully, he thought that the same thing would succeed in twins. His reasoning was that twins born from one mother's egg had their bodies produced from the identical material that wasn't a foreign or different tissue and couldn't be rejected. With that principle, an organ taken from an identical twin would survive in the other twin since they were innately the same. In Auschwitz, he devised a plan to damage the kidneys of one twin with poison and then transplant a healthy kidney taken from his or her twin sibling. The transplants were successful in identical twins, but most of the victims died because of botched surgery or infection. Those who survived the longest following the surgery died from starvation and the deplorable sanitary conditions that caused infection for which no antibiotic treatments were available at the time. The Nazis praised Josef Mengele for the success of the experiments, and he was given credit for my uncle's inhumane work.

Reisbach was not discouraged because his mentor received all the recognition for his work and was proud of its success. He credited the best surgical results in those who had the ability to better tolerate the gas chamber. Those who lived the longest, he attributed to their tolerance to survive the poison gas Zyklon-B that was used in the death chambers. Following the war it was no longer produced because of its association with the death camps. By continuing to collaborate with his mentor, her uncle had hoped to develop Zyklon-B into a suitable form to be utilized as an anti-rejection drug for use in human transplantation surgery. He told her parents about his research and his goal to enter medical school in Germany after the war. Her mother was a nurse and was appalled that her diabolical brother-in-law might someday become a doctor. She considered him a heartless savage that deserved to die. Not unexpectedly, his plans changed when Germany lost the war and he had to escape to avoid being charged with war crimes. Mengele, who treated him like a son, went to Argentina, and her uncle followed him there.

Paul was flabbergasted by what he had heard. It confirmed what Karen had told him and filled in most of the details. Paul was curious about how they were able to avoid detection and escape. Margarita said the uncle was considered to have played a minor role in the atrocities committed during the war, and literally got away with murder since he hadn't attained the notoriety of the doctors like Mengele who at Auschwitz was known as the Angel of Death. Despite the doctor's reputation, he was able to travel throughout Spain disguised with a mustache and beard and accompanied by the uncle as his son. After the war, many Germans fled to Spain, since conditions there were better than in Germany. During wartime, Spain was a neutral country and did not experience the destruction and mayhem that Germany had encountered. Living there even with the post-war shortages was not as bad as in living in their fatherland. There were many shortages particularly gasoline, but the German black market helped their countrymen leave Spain for South America. With enough money, a car could be bought as well as a passport to travel as a Spaniard. Automobiles were available because they were mostly useless to the Spaniards who didn't have the money to buy gasoline. They sold their cars on the black market to buy food and other essentials. Everything was extremely costly, but the wealthy Germans who had escaped with money could live well in the country or flee to South America.

The most notorious war criminals who escaped, fled to Galicia in the isolated northwestern region of Spain and Mengele accompanied by Reisbach found their escape route to South America there. Galicia was a fascist haven after the Spanish revolution and General Franco's favorite place in all of Spain. The Nazis were welcomed there and moved about freely, and with a large port in Galicia, both escapees boarded a boat to South America. Argentina had alliances with Spain and Germany and early after the war welcomed the Nazis into their country without restriction.

Paul astounded by Margarita's story remarked that her uncle was a smart man who had to know some basic facts about genetics to do what he did. She was visibly shaken, and tremulous sobbing uncontrollably answered that her father's twin was evil, created and possessed by the devil. His warped mind only fed his sadism, and he helped no one. Her father was devastated knowing that he and his brother were cut from the same cloth and called him a merciless butcher with no sense of value for human life. It was a visit after the war when her father said he never wanted to see his brother and never saw or heard from his twin again. His depression worsened, and although he had never been religious, he began to pray to the saints of the Catholic church and strictly observed all its religious rituals. With the belief that his brother was either possessed by the devil or the devil incarnate, he devoted his life to praying for his salvation. After her mother had died, no one could console him, and he refused to eat, fasting every day and prayed obsessively while his physical appearance and hygiene were terribly neglected. In solitude and praying all day, he refused to speak to anyone, including his own daughter who he turned away. Refusing to get medical help, he'd point to the sky with his hands clasped in prayer, saying he was in God's hands.

Paul very sympathetically said, "You must have had a terrible time carrying this heavy burden by yourself after your mother's death."

Hoping that his show of empathy would melt away the resistance to telling them where her father was, he tried to explain how important it was to determine beyond a shadow of a doubt that he never fled from Spain. The only way they had to clear his name was by stopping his brother from continuing to pose as him and asked her if she really wanted the evil uncle to continue to live his life known as her father, a moral and holy man. He said to prove her dad's identity they would not have to move him from wherever he was, even if dead. They needed a DNA test to determine that he was the son who was the Luftwaffe pilot and never went to medical school or became a surgeon that murdered innocent people. All it required was a sample of his saliva or blood, and if he had died, there were methods for obtaining a sample even after death. The result would definitely show that her father's murderous brother was not him and whether dead or alive, he could never be accused of being a Nazi or for his brother's crimes.

Karen became impatient with the lengthy discussion in Spanish. Interrupting she addressed Margarita and asked, "Donde esta tu padre ahora?"

Paul couldn't believe that Karen knew enough Spanish to abruptly interrupt the conversation just as he was getting Margarita to disclose where her father was. Margarita, however, surprised Paul and relented telling him that to atone for his sins and those of his brother her father had joined a monastery and became a monk. Paul didn't completely understand what she had said and asked what she meant.

"What kind of priest?" he asked.

"No not a real priest. The type they call a monk or brother." Margarita answered.

Paul asked her directly. "What part of Spain is he in?"

She was still reluctant to give him that information, but she finally gave in and said, "He's in a Trappist Monastery in Andorra."

Karen barged in at full force, wanting to know what was said.

Paul answered, "He's a monk in Andorra."

"Where the hell is Andorra?" she impatiently wanted to know.

Paul shrugged his shoulders and didn't know. She brusquely told him to find out. He then informed her that he's a Trappist monk, and they don't speak to people.

Karen didn't pause for a breath before she said, "It really doesn't matter, all we need is his DNA."

Too embarrassed to appear ignorant by asking Margarita where Andorra was he wondered if there was a flight to Andorra from Barcelona. She smiled and realized he had no idea where it was. Drawing a rough map of Spain on a napkin, she outlined where Barcelona and Andorra were located. Looking at it, he saw that Andorra was close and bordered on Barcelona. She explained that it was only a few hours away.

As Paul paid for the meals, Karen thanked her profusely for her help and asked what monastery he was in. She said she didn't know because she hadn't seen him in several years and added that there were many monasteries in Andorra but the country is so small it shouldn't be difficult to find. As they were leaving the restaurant, he asked Margarita if there was anything she wanted them to tell her father.

Without hesitation, she said, "Yes, tell him that I'm still alive and would like to see him and connect with him in some way."

Chapter Eleven

Karen was ecstatic about finding a positive lead to the twin, but she didn't know anything about Andorra. After contacting the agency to get information on travel and the monasteries there, she decided to buy a map of Andorra. The small screen on her laptop didn't adequately display local geography to her satisfaction, so she went out to look for a shop that sold maps. Paul felt bad about not calling Clara, the girl from the census bureau. He hadn't talked to her since they had coffee at Starbucks. Finally calling after five PM, she was excited to hear from him and wanted to know what his plans were for that evening. Hearing that he couldn't see her that night and would be unavailable for a few days, was disappointing and she was curious about the reason. Work on an important assignment called for his leaving Barcelona in the morning, he replied. When asked where he was going, he hesitated to say more and answered that it hadn't been determined. Explaining that the company he worked for had made the travel plans, he wasn't told where he was going. That didn't make it any clearer and she questioned what company he was talking about. To eliminate further questions and keep the conversation brief, he said he believed they had plans to visit Andorra. Eager to be helpful, she told him that driving to Andorra took a couple of hours and the mountains on the way were breathtaking with spectacular scenery. Her friend who lived there would be happy to show him around. Paul thanked her but explained that he would only be spending a few days there on business and would not have time for sightseeing. Becoming increasingly apprehensive about saying more, he tried to end the conversation, but she insisted on giving him her friend's name and telephone number. Writing the name and number in a notepad on the nightstand next to the bed, he ended the discussion with a promise to call her on his return to Barcelona.

Karen returned from her search for a map and knocked on the adjoining door to see if he was in. She told him she wanted him to go over the route to Andorra with her. Her map reading was a bit rusty and flattered him by admitting that men were better at reading maps than women. After reviewing it with her, they understood how close Andorra was to Barcelona.

Taking her by surprise, he said, "It's a short ride, about two to three hours by car."

Suddenly he realized his slip of the tongue as she turned to him with a suspicious glance. Not wanting to explain what the source of his information was, he lied that it was on a Spanish website. Looking at the map, she became aware that driving through the mountains to find the locations of monasteries could be a problem, but there were no alternate means of travel. Complicating the driving was her fear of using a GPS that could easily be used to trace their activity. Flying there with an agency jet or commercial airline to search for monasteries was out of the question.

Interrogating him about his unexpected knowledge about the trip, she asked, "How did you learn how long it takes to drive to Andorra?" She snapped, "Why didn't you tell me sooner?"

All this from the internet, she questioned and suspected the information came from the census bureau clerk. He told her he had discovered a website about travel to Andorra. Taking out her laptop she asked him to find it for her. He hesitated and said that it was in Catalan, the Andorran language that's hard to understand. She was now convinced that he was lying and told him that most internet sites had translations in English. He began to look busy searching the web, and before he was going to say he couldn't find it, the phone rang. She answered, and it was her Barcelona connection confirming that their visas for the journey were ready. Fortunately, she forgot about the Spanish website, which avoided another embarrassing confrontation. Before retiring for the night, she called the front desk to have the rental car ready at the entrance of the hotel in the morning.

Karen decided that she'd drive until they were on the outskirts of Barcelona, and then give him the task of the driving while she looked at documents listing monasteries and their locations. During the ride, he enjoyed seeing how different the suburbs of Barcelona were from those of the States. There were no big strip malls, large drug stores, hamburger franchises or huge banks in the small towns and villages. He kept looking for a Starbucks but couldn't find one. Reflecting on the encounter with the gal in Barcelona, he compared it to casually meeting women in the States. In his mind, they were more spontaneous and approachable than women from New York.

After the first hour of driving, the scenery changed from relatively flat cultivated land to increasingly higher rock covered hills. They hadn't reached the highest elevations known for breathtaking vistas, and the route began to become winding, turning in every direction. The car took the curves with ease, and they were making good time. The outside temperature started to drop as they drove to higher elevations and the road narrowed to one lane in each direction. The mountainside seemed to extend to the inner lane of the highway with a short distance between the passenger seat of the car and the mountain wall. Reaching her hand out the passenger window, Karen could almost touch the stone edge from where she sat in the vehicle. Paul had difficulty maneuvering the car to avoid hitting the mountain wall while struggling to keep from crossing over into the oncoming lane. Fortunately, there weren't many cars on the road in either direction. The outer lane of the road was narrowly separated from the edge of a steep cliff ending several hundred feet below with only a low metal guardrail to stop a vehicle from careening off the side of the mountain. Karen saw that Paul was having difficulty steering and offered to take over the driving, but there wasn't a place to stop safely and change drivers. She stopped studying the documents on her lap and nervously fixed her eyes on the road to periodically remind him to slow down around the curves and keep to the inner roadway. Suddenly, they were startled by two loud, high-pitched popping sounds ringing out from the rear of the vehicle that seemed like gunshots or blown-out tires followed by a sudden blast of released air. Before she could decide what had happened, Paul lost control of the car, and with a deafening bang, the auto hit the shoulder of the mountain. Attempting to stop the auto from veering into the outer roadway, he realized that the brakes had failed. Furiously and repeatedly pumping the brake pedal, while trying to maintain the vehicle on the inner lane, the car rebounded onto the oncoming path adjacent to the cliff's edge. Totally out of control, it sped toward a hairpin turn with nothing to obstruct its path and prevent the vehicle from plunging into the ravine below. Petrified, they pictured the car lurching off the edge, plummeting downward. As they realized they were about to die, an old truck suddenly appeared from the other direction smashing into the passenger side of the car. Their vehicle immediately stopped advancing forward towards the edge of the cliff and plunged sideways down the road. Following the collision, the truck overturned stretched out on its side at the curve in the outer lane with its rear end dangling over the edge of a precipice, tottering and ready to fall into the gulch below.

On impact, Karen's airbag inflated, pushing her to the driver's side of the car which blocked Paul's ability to see what was happening. Dazed, he wasn't sure if his door would open or if it did open he'd fall out into the ravine. Pushing Karen's airbag away from him, he tried to exit from her door and saw that Karen was unconscious. He checked her carotid pulse and found it beating rapidly. Reaching the inside handle of the passenger door to force it open, Paul crawled over Karen and dragged her out to the road. She resisted, struggling while he pulled her to the ground. Disoriented, she gazed around but didn't seem to grasp what had happened. He checked her skull for fractures and noticed a bump the size of a large egg on her outer right forehead. She was moving all her limbs, and her pupils were equal. While examining her, he heard moaning coming from the truck. Finding the person in the cabin of the truck who groaned was dangerous as it had flipped on its side with the wheels and floorboard facing Paul. Struggling to reach the driver's window, he leaned against the rusted metal body of the truck and looking into the driver's cab realized his weight against the door could push the vehicle off the cliff. Unable to see anyone from his vantage point, he hesitated to hoist himself higher out of fear of toppling the entire vehicle into the chasm below. Pulling the driver out from the window or door was not an option. He called out to see if anyone would answer and only heard moaning that came from the front compartment of the vehicle. He saw that Karen was attempting to sit up and shouted for her not to stand. She seemed oblivious, so he went over to move her closer to the truck to keep an eye on her. He inspected the old dented and rusted truck, believing that he might reach the man through the corroded floorboard that had been almost entirely replaced with wood that was rotting. With the truck's underside facing him, he looked through the cracks in the floorboard and didn't see anyone. Grabbing his jacket from the car and wrapping it around his right hand, he began ripping away the rusty metal and rotted wood. In the cab, he saw the elderly driver lying on the other side of the compartment with his head against the door window. The man continued to groan and didn't respond to Paul's instructions in Spanish. Karen in the interim appeared to recover her senses and got up to help him.

They both removed part of the floor of the front compartment making a hole large enough to reach in and get to the driver. Seeing that he was a small thin man, they were able to grab his legs and pull him through to the ground. Karen tried to call an emergency number, but there was no service. She remembered that approximately a half an hour earlier they had passed a small town. One of them would have to walk to get help in the village. Since Paul was attending to the unconscious man, she had to do it. Examining the old man, he found several broken ribs but no skull fractures, but he did notice that one of his pupils was larger than the other and suspected more than a simple concussion. He was concerned that the man had suffered a cerebral hemorrhage and would have brain damage from blood pressing on his brain. If it was arterial bleeding, his survival was a race against time.

As she prepared to walk to the village, a car approached from the opposite direction on the outer roadway that was blocked by the overturned truck. It stopped in time to avoid a collision and appeared small enough to pass around the wreckage. Karen walked over to the driver and asked him to get help in the next town and inform the police of the accident. After the car had passed, she went to help Paul as he monitored the truck driver who was now comatose and had stopped moaning. He was concerned that the longer they waited for help to arrive, the man's chance for recovery worsened. Although she was shaken by the accident, she realized that it would have been a far worse crisis without Paul's help. He impressed her with his control of the disaster that could have killed them. She then went to check their rental car and saw large holes in both rear tires. As she had suspected, they weren't created by blow-outs and were likely shot out. The question in her mind was where the gunman had found a concealed spot on the narrow road that didn't have enough footing to hide and shoot from.

Paul was discouraged by the lack of improvement of the old man and questioned whether the people that Karen had spoken to had stopped for help at the next village. Desperately trying to call for help with his cell phone, he didn't have any service. He hadn't had much time to think about the accident, but the delay was getting to him. Pacing back and forth mumbling words of regret and feeling helpless in the face of an emergency, an hour elapsed before he spotted a car coming up the mountain toward them. Two men were visible in the car as it pulled up to the wrecked rental. The older of the two introduced himself as the local police chief and told them an ambulance and crew were on their way. He asked to see their passports, while the other man placed caution signs and barriers on the road. Both men recognized the truck driver lying comatose on the ground and called to him. There was no answer, and the younger man explained that it was his brother-in-law, Rodrigo. He said Rodrigo was a carpenter and handyman and was probably on his way to help with a home repair or work at a construction site. The police chief's name was Serrano. After asking Paul and Karen where they were headed, he saw that Paul was anxious about the man in a coma and remarked that the old man would not survive even if an ambulance had arrived earlier to bring him to a hospital. Paul asked why, and the answer was that the old mountain folks were just left to die since there were no local specialists or sophisticated medical facilities in the mountains. The only hope for survival was in Barcelona, which was two hours away. Paul inquired about taking him to Andorra for treatment. The chief replied that medical care for treating life-threatening brain injuries in a man of Rodrigo's advanced age was limited in Andorra and he would not survive. The ambulance and the crew finally arrived, blocking the entire road.

The chief asked them to accompany him to the police station in town to complete the paperwork for the accident report. Karen asked if he or his assistant could drive them to Andorra to finish the report since it was on their way and less than an hour away. Serrano advised them rather abruptly that if they refused to go to the local station, he would arrest them, and they would spend the night in jail. Since Karen didn't want the cops to find out that she was an FBI agent, she decided to cooperate even though the agency had to be notified as soon as possible about the incident to determine how the tires were blown out, and the brakes failed.

At the police station, they filled out the necessary accident forms, and Serrano questioned them further about their travel plans. He wanted to know who they were visiting and what their business was in Andorra. The police chief advised them that whoever it was they were calling on, had to meet them at the border since he didn't have the authority to enter Andorra and bring them to their destination. Paul pulled Karen aside to explain what Serrano, who only spoke Catalan-Spanish had said. She told Paul to advise him that dropping them at the border was all that was needed and warned him not to say anything about possibly being picked up by an FBI contact. However, Paul explained that the chief wanted the name of a person and a telephone number to call if any issues arose about the accident. He had told Paul that cell phones were unreliable in the mountains and to contact them in Andorra, he would only accept a person's landline number. She told Paul to give him the phone number of the hotel. Paul said that Serrano wouldn't take it and stressed he would only accept one belonging to the individual who was meeting them at the border and was responsible for them while they were there. Paul had tried to assure him that they'd be safe on their own, but Serrano insisted that he wouldn't release them without the name of the person who they were visiting and the host's phone number. Paul explained it to Karen, and they were stumped by how they would handle the matter. Giving the chief the name of an FBI contact would blow the case and she didn't even know if there was an FBI contact in a country as small as Andorra. They couldn't give him a straight answer and realized they were screwed. Paul reached for his wallet to search for the number that Clara had given him which he had scribbled on the hotel notepad. Handing his handwritten note to the police chief, Karen looked at him and wondered what was happening. She tugged on his shirt to find out what was going on. While the police chief jotted down the number Paul in a hushed voice told her what he had done. She couldn't believe that he had spoken to the girl in Barcelona again and revealed where they were going. Furious, her face turned beet red and her temper flared, the immediate response would have been to beat him to a pulp but fearing a confrontation that would end with a jail sentence, she displayed maximum restraint. She decided it wasn't the time or place for retribution. Serrano claimed there was no name on the paper that Paul had handed him. As beads of sweat formed on Paul's forehead, flustered because he couldn't immediately recall Clara's friend's name, he wasn't sure what it was. Struggling with his memory, the name although uncertain came to him, he gave it to the chief who went to his office and called to arrange the meeting. While the police chief was in his office on the phone, Karen lashed out at Paul telling him they were probably targeted because of his irresponsible telephone call to the Spanish girl who she had seen him with in the Starbucks in Barcelona. After apologizing, he wondered what telling their destination to the girl had to do with the crash from tire's blowing out and, whispered if he had not gotten the phone number from the gal, they'd be in jail. She then revealed that the tires didn't blow out they were shot out.

His face turned pale gray as the beads of sweat streamed down his face. An assassination attack he repeated in a whisper! With a painful look of frustration, she nodded in the affirmative as Serrano returned and looked at them wondering what had happened. Even though incensed with Paul, she grabbed his arm to steady him as he appeared about to keel over. The chief was concerned about him and rather than taking them to Andorra offered to find a place in town for them to spend the night. They thanked him but said it was unnecessary. The chief believed Paul's appearance was a delayed reaction from the shock of the accident and refused to take them anywhere unless they had something to eat before leaving. They had only eaten breakfast, and it was an easy decision for them to accept his offer. After the meal, he drove them to the Andorran border. Serrano left Karen alone in the car while he walked with Paul to look for Clara's friend who had promised to vouch for them. Karen had tried to explain to the chief that they had never met the lady, and she was only a friend of a friend. Afraid that Paul alone might not be able to identify the woman and couldn't make the connection, their plan would be ruined. Her plea was ignored by the chief whose grasp of English was poor, and he insisted she remain in the car since Paul was the one with woman's name and number. As Paul entered the waiting area, he was thunderstruck by a stunning beauty in a flaming red dress who sat alone. She was as exquisite as a Hollywood starlet, and the most dazzling beauty his eyes had ever beheld. Trying to restrain his excitement, he quietly approached her and introduced himself as Clara's friend and apologized for the inconvenience they were causing her. She politely answered that it wasn't a problem since she had expected his call. They walked to the car, and Paul introduced her to Karen, who was now reassured that they were on the right course. Serrano in a proper authoritarian tone warned them that in Andorra, their new friend was responsible for them until all the legal and insurance issues of the accident were settled. The gal answered that she understood, and it was her pleasure to invite them to her home and treat them as part of her family. Finally, the chief released them, and they drove away in Angela's tiny Fiat. Angela asked if they wished to spend the evening in her apartment until they had a better idea of what Andorra had to offer for lodging. Karen explained that they had reservations at a hotel, and it was not necessary. She drove them to the hotel, and they thanked her repeatedly and she said she would call in the morning to see if they needed anything. Karen couldn't believe how thoughtful the gal was and could only imagine what Paul had promised the girl in Barcelona. All the while Paul could only think of the gorgeous gal in the red dress and was smitten with her beauty and delightful charm.

They checked into the hotel and had the same adjoining room arrangement that they had in Barcelona. She warned him not to make any calls without clearing them with her, and he agreed. Her call to Barcelona for a heads up on an FBI contact in Andorra confirmed that there was no one locally connected with the FBI and Barcelona was the only place to call if she needed help. She described what had happened and wanted someone from the bureau to check the wrecked car before the rental company had it repaired. Confident that it wasn't an accident, her conclusion was they were targeted to make it appear as a fatal accident on a treacherous road. Exactly how the car was sabotaged was unclear, but she added whoever did it was an expert. She hung up the phone and tried to relax but became aware of the painful bump on her head and the pounding headache that accompanied it that was getting worse. Paul knocked on her door to see how she was feeling and told her that they should ask the front desk for the location of the nearest hospital with a CAT scanner to examine her with a brain scan.

Karen said that she was okay and only needed ice for her head and called the front desk for ice. He stressed that a neurologist should examine her to be certain it was just a mild concussion before they started looking for the monk. He explained that it wasn't a lengthy examination and would only take a few minutes. She answered that she wasn't going to a hospital and told him if he was so concerned maybe he could check her since it would take less time than being examined in an emergency room. Surprised by her response, he began testing her balance by having her walk back and forth in the hallway. Her pupils reacted to light and were symmetrical. Although he didn't have a reflex hammer to check her reflexes, improvising using his hand and fingers to tap on her knee had to suffice. Sliding his left hand under her thigh to position her knee for the test, she suddenly pulled away. That wasn't the reflex he had expected. He told her he was going to check her reaction to a Babinski test, and she laughed saying it sounded like something you ordered in a delicatessen. He chuckled and told her it was the name of the doctor who discovered the test. It was the first time he'd seen her laugh during the entire trip, and it made her more appealing. After finishing the neurological exam, he approached her to examine the lump on her head. Again, she turned her head away as he moved in closer to inspect it. She blushed and was embarrassed by her reaction. The bump didn't seem any larger, but her response puzzled him. He didn't know what she thought he was about to do. Touching the bump hurt and reassuring her that it was necessary to check if the swelling had changed didn't seem to correct her level of discomfort with the examination. The nearness of his face to hers, and his hands touching her forehead seemed a bit too close and intimate for her. All during the trip, she had tried to maintain a professional distance that prevented any touching or close contact with him and had no recollection of his examination of her on the road after the crash. All the while he couldn't help but think that a Spanish girl would not have been as uneasy about touching her forehead or grabbing her knee. It confirmed his impression that American women avoided close contact because they had intimacy issues and didn't trust men. The ice had arrived, and Paul said he'd check on her during the night. He reassured her that it was needed to determine any change in her level of consciousness. She thought it was unnecessary but thanked him for his attention. To impress her with the seriousness of her injury, he told her that people died following head trauma because they weren't adequately followed up. Her main concern was that being awakened periodically during the night would affect the alertness and focus they would need the following day and interfere with her plan to visit monasteries. Losing some sleep didn't bother him, but she was exhausted and called room service for dinner. While waiting for dinner, she booked a rental car for the morning.

Following a shower in his room and relaxing on the bed, he heard someone in the hallway by her door. He assumed it was the waiter with their dinner and went to her room to let him in. She had just finished showering and walked out of the bathroom with her body wrapped in a towel. Observing several bruises on her leg, upper chest, and shoulder, Paul suggested that he check her for broken bones. She refused claiming that her only pain was a headache and was sure that nothing was broken. He didn't persist, thinking it would make her uncomfortable and ruin the relaxed moment they were having. While they talked about the day's events, she emphasized that someone had followed them and they had to be ready for any eventuality. She had not rented a car with a GPS, and they would have to depend on a map and compass to not be detected while exploring Andorra. Joking that in New York City, a compass wasn't needed to get around, he had never learned to use one. She laughed and said in Idaho, using a compass was a necessity that was taught in school, but Andorra wasn't covered in world geography class. He smiled, and even though they hadn't had any wine or liquor to drink, the atmosphere had become very relaxed. While they ate and talked, his eyes were on her loosening robe. It didn't leave much to his imagination, and he could picture her voluptuous body within it. Making a move on her was very tempting, and from his demeanor with his eyes exploring her body, she was aware of his growing sexual interest in her. As they finished eating, she was rather abrupt and told him they should relax in their rooms and get some sleep.

He went to his room, turned on the television and collapsed on the bed. He wasn't very sleepy as his mind wandered through the day's events. Eventually, he thought about dinner in her room, the robe, and her body and couldn't get the image out of his mind. Dwelling on her voluptuous body and her freshly showered scent, he became sexually aroused. He needed a distraction and began thinking about his wife and kids. He had not called them while in Spain and could imagine what Maria was thinking. The thought should have cooled down his passion, but it didn't seem to help. In parochial school as a teenager, the nuns taught them that prayer would squelch any carnal desire. He knew it didn't work then, and it wasn't going to work now. He recognized the task of examining her during the night would require a professional attitude but seeing her in a semi-naked state had made him horny, which was something he had never experienced before with female patients. Karen was no different than any other patient, but even the nuns who taught in parochial school would have agreed that being exposed to her gorgeous body every day would be what they considered an occasion for sin. While he struggled to figure out how to handle his dilemma, he heard the rattling of keys and saw the doorknob on the hallway door turning. He sat up in bed in a panic and thought of Karen's warning about assassins.

He ran to a side of the room away from the door and shouted in Spanish, "Who's there?"

The nighttime maid reassured him that she was only there to turn down the bed and freshen up the room.

Still uncertain, he cracked the door open and whispered, "No gracias."

Feeling as though he'd been blindsided by a three hundred pound linebacker with his legs ready to give out, any carnal desire he had quickly dissipated, and he was overcome with exhaustion. His thoughts turned to Maria, and his kids and he felt like a real jerk about how he reacted with the young woman he had met in Spain, and now Andorra. Even the sexual feelings that Karen aroused in him began to bother him. What was happening, he wondered? He thought he was acting like a teenager with fantasies that could never be fulfilled. In his youth, they were great and made him feel alive, but now he felt foolish. The more he thought about it, the more he believed being released from his wife's clutches and the rigor of his chosen profession gave him an unbridled sense of freedom. He no longer was experiencing the night terrors and sleep paralysis he had in the States and the thought of returning to face his problems distressed him.

Karen reflecting on their encounter that evening, thought she had allowed too much freedom of his hands on her body. Although exhausted, she should have gone to the hospital to be examined. His warm hands on her body had a gentle and almost timid affect and was so sweet as compared to guys she had dated who fondled her with their rough hands as though they were throwing a basketball or football to score a point or touchdown. She wasn't sure how she would react when he was sneaking in her room that night to inspect the bump on her head and wake her out of a sound sleep. She hoped it wasn't anything more than a tap on the shoulder and a reminder to open her eyes. Anything more might cause a mindless reaction, pulling him into the bed with her. The idea frightened her, but she dismissed it as foolishness. She told herself that she was neither young nor impetuous and her emotions were under control, even the powerful erotic ones. Reminding herself that the object of her mission was to find her father's killer and not a Latin lover, she tried to doze off.

Her mind refused to shut down, and it returned to his examination of her reflexes without a warning of what was to be expected. She thought it was entirely out of character for him. Socially he appeared self-conscious and shy, but he had no hesitation grabbing her thigh. Was it an erotic interest in her? His hands weren't cold as though he was restraining himself from doing something objectionable. It was more like a clinical thing that he was trained to do and hadn't given any thought to it while examining her. She hoped that he would explain the maneuver to other women before they were tested that way. Was she a prude and shrew she wondered? She really didn't know and couldn't decide since no other man had touched her in a while. Would she allow him to get intimate with her? She really didn't want to think about it anymore and finally fell asleep.

Chapter Twelve

Even though he hadn't set the alarm, he remembered to wake up periodically and check her neurological status. The swollen lump was shrinking, and she was alert each time he awakened her. There was no intimacy during the early morning hours since their only desire was to sleep. In the morning, they ate in the hotel and during breakfast acted as though nothing had happened the prior evening. Her headache had disappeared, and she looked and felt well. Following the morning meal, he had received a call from Angela, the woman they met at the border, who had checked to see if they needed anything and offered to give them a tour of Andorra. He declined the offer claiming they had work to attend to all day. However, she showed up at the hotel surprising them as they were preparing for their day trip to find a monastery. While getting dressed for work, Angela had received a call from Serrano who was looking for Paul. He wanted him to call him ASAP and wouldn't leave the message with her. The police chief didn't tell her what Paul had to call him about but mentioned the truck driver Rodrigo had died. When she broke the news to them,

Paul remembered that the police chief predicted the death. Suddenly he began to feel responsible for not providing the necessary care for Rodrigo at the scene of the accident and leaving his care in the hands of the local medics. The truck appearing on the road at that moment in time saved their lives and a few seconds earlier or later, they would have plunged off the mountain to their deaths. A terrible feeling of guilt swept over Paul as he reflected that Rodrigo's life was sacrificed to save them. He looked at Karen to see how she was reacting to the report of the truck driver's death. There were no outward signs of shock or sorrow, and she appeared more concerned about returning Serrano's call. She was one tough cookie who emerging unscathed by terrible events and death, made it uncomfortable for him to work with her. He contended that deep inside her, there had to be a glimmer of sentiment since the old man had died while they survived. For Karen, though, it was business as usual as she turned to him to urge him call the police chief immediately and check to see what was going on. Angela again, offered to help them see the sights, explaining that it wasn't a problem for her to take the day off from work.

Karen yelled out to Paul in English, "Get rid of her now and call Serrano!"

Approaching the Andorran beauty, he noticed how alluring she appeared simply dressed in a blouse and jeans. Calmly fixing his eyes on her, he told her that they really appreciated all her help but could not get her involved with their business. They were meeting with people who would object to her presence and he said, the meetings were boring, and the people and discussions dull. That seemed to placate her, and Karen smiled as she got the gist of their conversation. Angela didn't leave while Paul called the chief to ask if there was anything he could do for the truck driver's family. Serrano said Rodrigo only had a sister and sending money for a proper burial would be appreciated.

The police chief got down to business and wanted to know,

"What are you really doing in Andorra?"

Paul asked, "What do you mean?"

Serrano explained, "The accident was not simply blown out tires. It was caused by strategically placed explosive devices wired to a GPS and controlled from a remote device. The explosion was planned to go off on the road at that exact moment, and unfortunately, Rodrigo got in the way before it could finish off the two of you."

Shocked by what he heard, he attempted to maintain control of the conversation by keeping the police chief in the dark about their trip to Andorra.

In a strained voice, he said, "We didn't think it was an explosion, it sounded like two blowouts or maybe gunshots."

Trying to sound dumbstruck he bellowed, "I can't understand why anyone would want to do that to us!"

Serrano told him, "Cut the crap and level with me."

Paul answered, "I have no idea what's going on, but I'll ask Karen about the car rental and the possibility that we got the wrong car from the rental company and the attack was meant for someone else."

Trying to hold back from saying too much, he told the chief of police that he'd get back to him after he discussed it with Karen and hung up. Serrano called back immediately and heated, warned him that they would be jailed if they were withholding information from him. Attempting to further frighten Paul, he commented that Spanish prisons were worse than death sentences and they would rot in jail for years awaiting a trial date to be set. Attempting to sound confident Paul replied that he understood, and he had no fear of being sent to prison since they didn't know why the car would have had explosives or if the blast was meant for them. Never the less, he was frightened by the remarks and turned to Karen for help with the police chief.

Angela saw he appeared unsettled by the call and asked in Spanish, "What's wrong?"

Not revealing what had alarmed him he said, "I'm upset about Rodrigo."

She sat next to him to comfort him, and Karen gave them a contemptible look suggesting that he should quit the nonsense and regain his composure.

Angela was rubbing his shoulders while Karen stared at them in disgust and would have let out a deafening stream of profanities if they weren't in a hotel lobby. Completely captivated by Angela's warmth, he seemed to be in a hypnotic trance and forgetting about the depressing telephone call, could only think of bedding her. Karen interrupted their romantic encounter and thanked her for volunteering to help but told her that they had to get on with their work.

In a whisper, he told Angela, "I'll call you for dinner when we're finished with the meetings."

Karen had sandwiches and beverages prepared from the hotel kitchen while waiting for a rental car to be brought to the hotel. Deciding to drive, she was confident they wouldn't get lost, although Paul wasn't sure she knew where they were going. Driving about two blocks from the hotel, Karen stopped at a service station. Paul thought she had stopped for gas, but she told him to ask the attendant to put the car on a rack and hoist it. He didn't question her and asked the attendant to set the auto on the lift in the garage. The attendant looked at them wondering what the crazy Americans were up to. Paul handed the guy a couple of dollars and told him to do it. As soon as the car was up on the lift, she began inspecting the underside of the vehicle checking the brakes and axles. Satisfied there was no evidence of tampering, and no hidden devices, they drove away.

Impressed by her performance, Paul said, "I don't know too many women who can inspect the underbelly of a car and know what they were looking at."

She answered, "You don't know many women from Idaho."

Paul smiled and asked, "Where are we going?"

Pointing to the glove compartment, she said, "Take out the map and find a town called Canillo."

She seemed rather cold and distant, and he realized she was still mad about Angela hanging around the hotel earlier.

Ignoring her mood, he asked, "What's in Canillo?"

"There's an abbey there run by nuns of the Trappist order in honor of the patron saint of Andorra, the Virgin of Meritxel," she replied.

She derisively added, "It's the home of a virgin which is a terrific place for you to visit and quell your obsession with Spanish women."

They both laughed, but in a serious vein he asked, "Why would he be living with a bunch of nuns?"

She answered, "If the authorities were after him they'd never think of searching in a cloister full of nuns?"

He didn't respond and decided to take in the sites which he found rather ordinary after Barcelona except for the magnificent mountains that they narrowly escaped death from. The architecture compared to Barcelona was monotonous with the uniform façade of brown or grey stone. Fortunately, it was a quick ride twelve miles away from the hotel and less than thirty minutes without traffic. He asked her if they had an appointment and she told him they were meeting with Mother Antonia Caterina.

They parked the car and began searching for the central office. As they walked towards a chapel, all the buildings appeared alike casting a monotone grey atmosphere. Paul remarked that Gaudi apparently had not designed the abbey. The chapel didn't stand out from the rest of the stone buildings, and they approached a monk to ask directions to the Mother Superior's office. He guided them by signaling with a hand gesture to follow him and they were taken to small structure across from the parking lot. The monk didn't say a word, and they assumed he was a Trappist who observed the vow of silence. The stone entrance to the building appeared the same as the other structures with no religious adornments or sculptures other than a small statue of the Virgin for whom the abbey was named. Entering a small lobby, there was a giant mural of the Last Supper on the wall surrounded by religious artifacts. Mother Antonia Caterina introduced herself and didn't have the stiff comportment of a Mother Superior that they had anticipated. She looked rather young and guessing her age was difficult. The black habit obscured most of her body only exposing her eyes, nose, and mouth. They couldn't see her hairline; however, her skin was pale ivory without a wrinkle or blemish. She didn't look like a modern American nun, but her mannerisms and facial expressions were warm and youthful and not defined by her severe black attire. Paul made the introductions in Spanish, but the Mother Superior quickly interrupted him in perfect English and said she knew who they were. Mother Antonia noted that they seldom had distinguished visitors from America and got up to show them the abbey. Looking at Paul, she said that she had heard he was a doctor who had taken the trip to Andorra to write a story and added that it must be important. He was ashamed to lie to a nun, especially a Mother Superior but answered that it was an extraordinary biography of an American surgeon and justified being away from his practice.

"The surgeon must be a great man," she responded and added, "In Andorra, doctors are not that famous or have enough spare time for writing stories."

She asked them, "How can I help you?"

Karen quickly answered that they were looking for a monk who was in Andorra and has a daughter in Barcelona and a twin brother in the United States whom they were writing about. Mother Antonia told her that there were only three monks who worked at the abbey and none of them had relatives in the United States or a daughter. Karen clarified it by adding that they weren't just interested in her convent but also other Trappist cloisters in Andorra. The nun answered that there was a monastery belonging to the Deus Rei affiliation where the rites of asceticism were strictly observed and included the vow of silence. She said the Monsignor there spoke English and supervised the monks who strictly obeyed their oath, and he might be able to help them. They thanked her, and Karen asked if she could call the head of the monastery for them and request an interview. The Mother said that she had never gone there or spoken to him, and they seldom saw outsiders, especially women, but she would try to arrange a meeting. In passing, the nun mentioned that one of the brothers from the Abbey occasionally helped at the monastery and could direct them to the location.

She picked up the phone and called to have brother Ignacio come to her office. Paul with a baffled glimpse at Karen wondered how a monk who didn't speak a word would be able to help them. Mother Superior saw the expression on his face and realizing the paradox it suggested, answered that he wasn't one of the silent ones. Brother Ignacio was there in less than a minute, and the nun asked him to describe where the monastery was located. It was the same monk who without saying a word showed them to the chapel and now answered in Spanish. He told them it was close to the border of France with Spain in a town called Arinsal. She asked him to give them directions, but he hesitated, telling her that the monastery was not in the village and the entrance was concealed and trying to find it was difficult. It was isolated and located about four to five kilometers off the main road. He described the street leading up to the path towards the monastery as steep, uphill and unpaved and the pathway a three kilometer long trail that was impossible to navigate without a four-wheel drive vehicle. The way was obscured by surrounding trees and wild bushes along the unpaved street and almost impossible to find. Mother Superior offered to have the monk show them where the road was, however, they weren't driving the right type of vehicle. Karen thanked her and asked if the brother could take the time to show them where the town was and the road that he had described. The nun explained that nothing was far away in Andorra and brother Ignacio could go with them and return with enough time to complete his chores. Before she dismissed the monk, it occurred to Mother Superior that he knew Monsignor Muller, the head priest, and could arrange the meeting for them. The nun offered to show them the abbey, but Karen declined since she was eager to lease a four-wheel auto before the rental shop closed for its siesta. The nun offered to have them stay for lunch, and Karen tried to politely talk her way out of prolonging the visit.

Unsuccessful at refusing the Mother Superior's invitation, they remained for a large meal that was the main repast of the day for the nuns. They discussed the history of the religious order and their daily routine that revolved around prayer. They learned that the sisters managed a farm growing fruit and vegetables and had several goats and a cow. The monks were there to assist the nuns and to travel to the town for the necessary supplies and staples. Money was earned from sewing religious garb for the church and other devotional articles to wear. It was almost three o'clock when Karen explained that they had to return to Val Del Andorra, the principal city in Andorra, to take care of unfinished business. She asked Mother Superior if brother Ignacio could show them where the Deus Rei monastery was located.

He joined them in their rental car and told them not to rent a four-wheeler that late in the day since the monastery was closed to outsiders while the monks began evening prayers and prepared for dinner. He'd take them to the dirt road leading to the path, and after an appointment was arranged to see the Monsignor, he would call them. Looking at their car, he said it would never make it on the steep path up the mountain to the monastery. He claimed the trail was obstructed with boulders and covered with large stones and rocks that could wreck the tires and transmission.

They reached the village called Arinsal and, it appeared practically deserted with empty restaurants and many of the shops and lodgings closed. Paul asked why the town looked abandoned and Ignacio explained that it was bustling during the skiing season but in the summer, it slowed to a complete stop. The summer visitors mainly used the ski slopes that were the highest in Andorra primarily on the weekends to hike and climb. The paved roadway ended at a vacant ski resort with a ski lift that stretched over the road. A narrow dirt street leading from the main thoroughfare advanced steeply up the west side of the mountain, and Paul found he had to shift into low gear as the car slowly crawled up the incline. They made the four to five kilometers to a spot covered by trees that hid the dirt pathway to the monastery and from there, it was difficult to see the monastery. Ignacio pointed to the path in the distance that twisted and turned as it moved uphill. The surrounding vegetation was heavily overgrown and verdant green as the summer months had melted the snow. The mountains beyond them revealed the gray granite peaks that glistened with a blue hue from the sun's reflection. Although the stone was the same color as the buildings in the village, it appeared alive in the bright sunlight. The view of the valley and mountain tops with the melting snow was spectacular and appeared to be only steps away from heaven.

After they had inspected the area, they drove the monk back to the abbey. On the way there, Karen was curious about the monk's life and his work in the convent. He explained that he and two of the other monks were needed to perform the tasks that the sisters couldn't handle. According to the friar, the nuns were often mechanically challenged and required help with everything from light bulbs to stalled tractors. Paul turned to Karen and quipped that apparently none of the sisters were from Idaho. Ignacio added that life in the mountains was a challenge, and most of the nuns were not from Andorra, but he didn't know if any were from Idaho.

In town, Karen drove to the car rental place to ask about a four-wheel drive SUV. To her dismay, there weren't any available. Although the ski season was over, the summer visitors who hiked trails and climbed mountains rented SUVs. The rental agent promised to call other agencies to find one for them. With no suitable autos available, he showed them the all-terrain vehicle rentals that he had available and took them to the back of his shop. Displeased to see that the ATVs looked no larger than a lawn mower with three or four wheels and a seat or two, she told him to find a four-wheel sedan or SUV before the morning, and she would pay whatever it cost to rent one. If there wasn't one in Andorra, she urged him to get one from Barcelona and he explained that would be difficult to arrange. She was frustrated, but Paul thought that maneuvering an all-terrain vehicle might be fun even though he had never ridden one. She looked at him in disbelief wondering why he didn't understand the problem and the shopkeeper left them alone to consider their options.

She lashed out at him saying, "Those vehicles offer no protection from a gunman and if we aren't shot at, we'll likely overturn one and break our necks."

They went directly to the hotel, and Karen called her Barcelona contact to ask about driving a Jeep or Range Rover to Andorra in the morning. It was too early for dinner and Paul decided to have a beer at the bar in the hotel lobby. Angela was on his mind, and he had promised to call her. He was having second thoughts about it when she suddenly entered the hotel. Restraining the impulse to walk over to her, he waved to her. When she arrived at the bar, he gave her a peck on the cheek. Delighted, she turned her mouth to his and gave him a big luscious wet kiss on the lips. Any hesitation he had about being with her rapidly melted away, and he asked where she wanted to have dinner. Relaxing about her second unexpected appearance at the hotel since the morning, he dismissed a paranoid thought that maybe she was setting a trap for him. Karen's repeated warnings about his brash behavior creating trouble had begun to bother him, but there was an attraction to the Andorran beauty that he couldn't resist. Angela persuaded him that there was no need to take her to a restaurant because she would cook a real Catalan meal for him in her apartment. He was getting nervous and began regretting the encounter. Apologizing that he had eaten a big lunch and Catalan cuisine was too rich for his unsophisticated American stomach, didn't seem to discourage her. She persisted by claiming that she was an excellent cook and he would enjoy a home cooked meal that would agree with him. She then went into a lengthy commentary about how and what she would cook for the meal and assured him that it was prepared with only the finest ingredients. Feeling he would appear ungrateful if he refused, he couldn't say no and accepted. She planned to pick him up at eight PM which was later than he usually had dinner but earlier than most Spaniards sat down for supper. He went up to his room to relax and called his wife who he hadn't called during the week.

His call got through, and the first words that greeted him were, "Where have you been?"

He responded with, "What do you mean?"

She said, "I've tried calling several times and always got a message that all the circuits were busy. It had never happened before when I called Puerto Rico."

"The weather has been lousy with tropical storms screwing up the telephone lines," he answered.

It had some truth to it since the summer was the rainy season in Puerto Rico. They talked politely for twenty minutes, and he then decided to get ready for dinner.

Angela picked him up at the hotel, and they drove to her flat, which was in a modern garden apartment complex in the outskirts of the town. It was a nicely furnished studio with some local art on the walls and soft, slow music coming from a stereo. She had opened a bottle of a hearty local red wine to let it breathe, and the aroma throughout the apartment from the food being prepared in the small kitchen made him yearn to return home to New York. He wasn't sure how to react to her hospitality and hadn't brought a gift in appreciation. Since she was Clara's friend, he decided to be reserved and detached with inane small talk over dinner. The meal was excellent, following which they polished off the remainder of the wine while relaxing on a couch in her apartment. In the background, the song playing was "Close Enough for Love." sung by a sensuous female vocalist.

Moving close to him with her arm raised on the back of the couch, he could feel the tips of her fingers brushing along his neck. The sweet scent of her perfume lingered in the air around her body creating a spellbinding aura. Things were moving faster than he had wished and not really knowing who she was made him feel uneasy. Indebted to her for getting them out of a tight situation he was becoming confused by her extraordinary hospitality and didn't wish to tarnish it with suspicion of her motives. He knew she worked as a secretary for a government official in Andorra but didn't know much else about her. Did she ply him with her sexual appeal for some ulterior motive that he would regret? She seemed to be genuinely passionate, but maybe all Spanish woman treated their men that way. He was trying to figure out what to expect and how to react but never in a situation like this with another woman, he was uncomfortable and definitely out of his league. He moved away a bit to distract her and temper his feelings by asking if she had ever been anywhere else besides Andorra.

She was surprised by the question but told him that she had seen most of Europe and lived in Barcelona while going to school and had remained there briefly to work. Her interests were not the same as most of the Barcelonans, and she decided to move back to Andorra where her roots were. Being primarily a small-town girl, she found the bustling city overly energetic with people so busy and preoccupied that it was very impersonal. Claiming with all the commotion and activity people in the city didn't have time for personal relationships or conversation. If they took time to speak to you, it was always a hurried discussion about the latest gossip in town, politics, sports, art shows and nothing about them or you. The men in Barcelona only talked about soccer and sex. Those were the only subjects they knew well. Here in Andorra, she described the people as friendly and one big family. During dinner, she had told him that she was an only child like him, and her parents had died, but with a lot of family in town, she was very close to her cousins.

He didn't understand how she differed from the woman in Barcelona and according to what she had told him the city appeared to be like New York city. Explaining that many of the people who live in New York describe Manhattan like that, he wanted to know what the men in Andorra were like.

"Do you prefer the men in your small country and how are they different than those in the big city that you didn't like?" he questioned.

She corrected him by saying she didn't dislike the city as much as living there. It was a great place to visit for entertainment, sports, art exhibits and the like but not to live there permanently. Men were the same in Andorra, but they're more robust and the outdoor type with big muscles from chopping firewood in autumn and clearing snow in the winter. They hunt, hike, ski or climb mountains depending on the season, but their personalities are the same as the men in Barcelona. They're not like me, Paul asked? She clarified it further saying that because they're like that didn't mean she disliked men. She admired their strength but was more interested in intelligence, and character. Machismo did not appeal to her and intelligence attracted her, especially in warm and sensitive men. She responded that she witnessed his reaction to the truck driver's death and because he couldn't help him it showed he was "molt simpatic" which translated from Catalan meant "muy simpatico" to him. She said it was the response of a man with enormous love in his heart.

It surprised him since it was the first time he had ever heard a woman use a line like that. He was taken aback by her boldness and said she really didn't know him so how could she say that. In New York, he'd be considered weak and effeminate to display a sentiment like that. In a way, he understood what she was trying to say because that's what he found most attractive about her. She was sensitive but not hysterical like some of the women he had known. He had to remind himself, that he really didn't know the woman and didn't want to create a major incident. His rationale shifted to one that convinced him that she wasn't entirely unknown since she was Clara's friend. Why was he questioning sweet innocent Clara's intentions for introducing her as though it was some plot to create trouble for him? After all, the only thing he had told her was that he was in Spain to get information to write a book, and there was no reason to be suspicious. He believed that he and Angela shared the same passion for each other and he couldn't resist her any longer. Moving closer and feeling her warm breasts pressing softly against his chest, he kissed her passionately on the lips. Being thoroughly entwined in her arms, there was a feeling of ecstasy that he never experienced before. It was an intoxicating drug that would become addictive and he accepted that. Aroused, he picked her up and carried to bed. Undressing her slowly, there was no resistance from her while he savored her body with his lips and hands. She became intensely aroused as her body became flushed and heated to an extreme ready to burst into flames. They made hot fiery love into the early morning hours, and it was beyond anything he had ever experienced before. Passionate, sensuous and unabashedly bold, Angela fulfilled his wildest dreams. Afterward, he hated to leave her but after a tender embrace and kiss, he called a taxi to return to the hotel.

At the hotel, he began to have regrets about acting so wildly uninhibited without any thought of self-control. His only feeling had been an exhilarating sexual desire that left him so excited that he couldn't fall asleep. He wanted to call to say how much the evening meant to him, but his blissful state of mind surpassed any words that could describe how he felt. Satisfied, she had to be feeling the way he did, he finally fell asleep.

Chapter Thirteen

Karen woke Paul up early to go to the car rental place. He was sleepy after his night with Angela and wanted to know what the rush was all about. She told him that she wanted to go over the plan for the day, particularly how to address the subject of Reisbach's twin with the Monsignor if the monk resides at the monastery. To gain the priest's cooperation and collect the monk's DNA sample, she wanted Paul to dress appropriately for the trip and meet her in the dining room for breakfast. He showed up in the hotel dining room wearing jeans and a T-shirt. Trying to remain patient, she asked if he planned to get dressed and he replied that he was dressed for the occasion. Upset by his answer, she advised him that the proper attire that a real doctor wore when trying to convince the head of the monastery, was not jeans and T-shirt. He reminded her that they were visiting ascetics living in the mountains who hadn't seen the outside world for eons and wouldn't know how a doctor dressed. He pointed out that riding in an all-terrain vehicle on a dirt road didn't require a suit and a tie. Calming down, she compromised, but insisted that he bring a jacket and shirt, so the Monsignor would more readily believe their charade. He grumbled and said he would change after breakfast but thought that formality was unnecessary in the mountains. They reviewed what they would say to the Monsignor and went to the auto rental agency. The agent explained that no SUVs had been returned the previous evening and after calling other agencies there were no SUVs available. After squabbling about an ATV, they agreed on one with two seats and hitched it to the car on a small trailer.

The ride to Arinsal was short lasting less than twenty minutes. They drove two to three miles on the unpaved road up the mountainside to the dirt path that led to the monastery. After leaving the car along the dirt road, they began the ride on the ATV, which was more difficult than they had anticipated. There were large stones some the size of small boulders obstructing the way that were difficult to avoid since the trail was surrounded by dense woods, thicket, and tall bushes on either side. The vehicle was old and required shifting to low gear on the incline and pumping the gas pedal to gain enough traction to maneuver past the obstacles. Nevertheless, Karen's ability to handle the ATV impressed Paul who was upset that he hadn't insisted on staying in jeans and a T-shirt. Both were covered in dirt and despite wearing goggles had difficulty with visibility. To avoid hitting surrounding trees and boulders, they removed the goggles frequently to clean the dust and dirt that accumulated from the trail. They had taken bandannas with them to cover their faces, but it didn't prevent dirt from caking in their mouth and nostrils. Rinsing with water to clean their mouth and nasal passages cleared away the caked mud and grime but slowed them down and wasted bottled water that they had taken with them to drink. Karen wasn't as disturbed about the muck as he was because she had grown up in the Northwest and was accustomed to dusty dirt trails. With the delays caused by stopping to attend to the goggles and bandannas, she worried that riding in a vehicle without the shielding of doors or a roof made them easy targets. The only weapon with them was a semi-automatic handgun that she brought, and her fear mounted as they were getting closer to the shelter of the monastery.

As they struggled with the ride on the path, the ATV hit a high stone ledge effectively blocking their way and with the trees and overgrown underbrush it was impossible to pass around it. Paul attempted to lift the front wheels over the rock as Karen pushed from the rear of the vehicle. Suddenly, gunshots rang out and Karen cried out to Paul to overturn the vehicle for cover and crouch down behind it. The gunfire was coming from the surrounding woods and aimed at them. It seemed to come from every direction as bullets ricocheted off the ATV, rocks, and boulders on the trail. Karen thought there might be more than one gunman. Trying to spot a shooter, she detected some movement between the trees and let loose with a round of ammunition and then waited. A volley of gunfire was returned from an automatic weapon in the location she had suspected. It was not only aimed at them as she realized the assailant was shooting at the vehicle's gas tank to explode it. Paul let out a sudden loud groan, and Karen saw that he had been hit by a bullet to the lower leg.

She was afraid they were sitting ducks about to be finished off when they heard barking dogs and gunfire coming from farther up the pathway. The barking was coming closer and the automatic fire ceased.

There was an eerie silence for a moment as four hooded monks carrying rifles approached from out of the woods behind them. The dogs were not with them and could be heard barking in the distance. One of the monks asked if anyone had been wounded, and Karen nodded yes. Paul said his leg was grazed, but he had stopped the bleeding with pressure. The tallest monk introduced himself as Monsignor Muller and spoke English with a slight British accent. He asked the other monks to check the woods across from them to see if anyone was wounded or dead. One of them returned with a rag soaked with blood, and the Monsignor told them to follow the trail of blood and the dogs. He then asked Karen and Paul if they were up to walking the rest of the way to the monastery since the ATV appeared in no condition to ride. He estimated that they were only a half a mile away from the monastery. As they began to walk, he explained that they had heard the gunfire and didn't think it was from hunters. Explaining that men in Andorra didn't use automatic weapons to hunt with, he was confident that it wasn't friendly gunfire. Karen was happy to be rescued but was surprised that the monks bore firearms. He explained that they were only used for hunting and life-threatening emergencies. Asking if any of the monks had ever shot and killed anyone, surprised him and the priest admitted that in the military before entering the priesthood, defending oneself involved killing the enemy. Studying him more closely, she guessed that he looked more like a rugged outdoorsman or ex-special forces military type rather than a priest, particularly one who was a Monsignor and the head of a monastery. His face was weathered with taut skin creased and tanned like old leather. The hair exposed from under his hood was light brown and not white as expected in someone who had reached the age of a Monsignor. Towering over them, with a height well over six feet, he didn't appear to be a Spaniard or from Northern Catalonia and spoke with a British twang. Paul asked him where he hailed from and was told that although Britain was his native land, he had lived in Andorra for eighteen years, and considered it his permanent home. Approaching the monastery, a gray stone building a few stories high, reminded Paul of an old New England college that had been erected centuries before.

There were many smaller buildings nearby with some constructed of wood, but most were granite structures. After they entered the monastery, Father Muller suggested they shower and provided them with robes to wear as their clothing was being cleaned. After showering, Paul returned while Karen spoke to the Monsignor and explained the reason for their visit to the monastery. She turned and glanced at him beaming with a big grin while holding back laughter and realized he looked absurd in a monk's garb. She sensed he wasn't in the mood for jokes after what they had just been through and remained silent. Bothered by their terrifying incident, and seeing her smiling and chatting with the priest, his sole impression was that she was one unperturbable broad.

They were almost killed, and she was standing there laughing with the Monsignor.

She saw the solemn expression of the drooped corners of his mouth and sadly lowered eyelids and attempting to lift his spirits said, "You look saintly in your robe; maybe you missed your calling."

The priest laughed and thought they were a cute couple and replied, "Laughter is good for the soul following adversity."

Troubled by the incident and without making it sound like an interrogation, Father Muller asked, "What are you really doing here?" and told them, "I don't believe the story about a biography."

He added, "No one shoots at biographers, especially when the book hasn't been written."

Karen came clean and told him she was an FBI agent, and Paul was a doctor who was helping with the investigation of his colleagues' murders. They wanted to interview the monk to establish that his twin in America, a surgeon, was a war criminal who worked in Auschwitz-Birkenau concentration camp with Doctor Mengele during World War Two and was also responsible for several murders in the States. The head priest not surprised by what he was hearing, looked at them with a pensive frown and warned that interrupting the prayers and silence of the monks would be difficult since they hadn't communicated with anyone from the outside world since they had entered the monastery and strictly obeyed their vow of complete silence. Karen asked if the monks would be able to answer questions by writing or typing on a computer keyboard. The priest explained that most of the monks were feeble old men easily frightened by new faces and technology and would have difficulty. He mentioned there was one elderly monk who fit their description but was near death from prolonged fasting that worried everyone in the monastery. Because of his age and poor health, he required an aide for bedside care and was so debilitated that the aide had to take him in a wheelchair to Mass and prayer gatherings. He didn't think he would be able to provide a written response since with severe malnutrition, he didn't have the strength to feed himself. The priest was concerned that Friar Heinrich, the monk that he was referring to and they were searching for didn't have much time left on earth. Muller had desperately tried to have local physicians examine him, but the monk refused and would probably refuse to cooperate with Paul. He concluded that he'd doubted that he'd agree to be seen by anyone but didn't want to discourage Paul if they could think of a way to persuade Heinrich. Karen tried to reassure the priest that Paul was a superb physician who specialized in internal medicine and would be able to convince the sick monk to be examined. She asked the priest if he was aware of the history of the Reisbach twins. The priest told her that every monk's background was thoroughly investigated before they were accepted for life in the monastery. He knew the history of Heinrich's military service and that of his twin. Because Muller had served in the army in Bosnia, he had a special interest in the friar and his brother. Before becoming a priest, he had witnessed the horrors of war and said Heinrich's reason for entering the monastery was not to avoid deportation or escape judgment for anything he did during the war. The monk entered to dedicate his life to God's service and sincerely believed that the sins of the world could only be forgiven by a life devoted to prayer in complete silence. He turned to them beseeching Paul to see if there was something he could do since Heinrich's lack of food and water during the past month had taken him to the brink of death and was about to kill him. Adding that the malnutrition was extreme to the point of death by starvation and it worried the other monks that Heinrich had a communicable disease like tuberculosis that they would contract.

Food was brought in for Karen and Paul to eat while they discussed with the Monsignor the need for a DNA test to verify the monk's identity. If they could speak to him, they could convince him to be examined because the remainder of the brothers in the cloister were demanding a specialist examine him to exclude a communicable disease that might kill them. While they were eating one of the monks, who had searched for the assailant entered and told Father Muller that the gunman had been found and was dead. Karen asked the monk how he had died thinking that one of the monks might have killed him. The monk responded that the man was wounded by Karen's gunfire and while trying to escape bled to death. She asked Monsignor Muller if they could examine the dead man and were accompanied to the room where the body had been placed. Paul immediately recognized the man as Kopchick, Doctor Reisbach's surgical assistant. Muller asked them if they knew who the man was, and Karen remarked that he was a nurse at Paul's hospital. She then asked the priest if they could see Reisbach's brother. He hesitated and said that he first wanted to talk to him and explain the reason for Paul's visit. To convince him to be examined, he believed it was necessary to first tell him that the other friars were very worried that he had a communicable disease that could spread throughout the monastery and kill all of them. They had wanted Muller to arrange for a doctor from Barcelona to assess Heinrich's condition, but now, he would tell them he had consulted a New York specialist. He said it was best to wait until the morning to reassess how to approach the sick holy man.

He had suggested that Paul and Karen spend the night at the monastery and complete the interview and testing with Heinrich in the morning. Karen objected and asked if one of the monks could accompany them to the road where the rental car had been parked. Muller explained that the monastery didn't have a vehicle to do that, and they would have to walk back. Paul complained that he couldn't walk that far with the bullet wound of his leg. Karen didn't think she'd find her way back to the hotel alone and they remained as the overnight guests of the monastery.

Chapter Fourteen

------◆◆◆------

The following day, the Monsignor talked to Heinrich while Karen and Paul remained outside the door of the monk's bedroom. The discussion was brief, and he asked them to come in the room to introduce them as the doctor and nurse from the United States. The monk's appalling resemblance to a cachectic prisoner of war or concentration camp detainee horrified them. His wasted features had almost no likeness to a living human being, and he appeared so unlike his brother that identifying him as the surgeon's twin from his facial features was impossible since he had the face of a skeleton. With a stooped body composed of skin and bones, he moved in his chair to shake Paul's hand with a weak right arm that he supported with his left hand. His effort failed as his forearm began to shake uncontrollably from a lack of muscle strength, and Paul grasped his hand and arm with both his hands to steady him. Gripping the limb, there was the strange sensation of flesh hanging and sliding over bone with no opposition from underlying muscle or fat. His body was literally skin and bones. Paul told Heinrich that he would remove his robe and cowl, to examine him more closely and

156

the monk nodded his head in approval. As he lifted the hood, he was shocked by the sunken eye sockets and protruding eyes staring into empty space as though gazing at the end of life. Paul recognized it as the death stare that occurred in terminal patients and the same look that he repeatedly witnessed in his nightmares; the waking dead now existed before him. As he checked the monk, he thought a strange electrical current was passing to him through his fingers as he touched Heinrich's skin. It alarmed Paul as it seemed to gradually increase, and he wasn't sure what the cause was or how to explain it. He could feel his inner body trembling as he tried to pull away but somehow couldn't because of a strange magnetic field. As the foreign energy charged every muscle in Paul's body with fine tremors, he lifted the friar from the chair to place him in bed. The monk was weightless, and the physician's hands could feel every spinal vertebra electrified as though he had energized rosary beads in his hands instead of the spine of a human. Disturbed by the weightlessness of his body and strange sensation that it released, Paul tried to maintain his clinical focus, and he struggled with his psyche to complete the examination. Estimating the friars weight to be no more than sixty to seventy pounds, he realized it was less than half that expected in an adult of his size and couldn't believe the monk was still alive. He tried to focus by remembering the degree of weight loss a human could tolerate before all bodily function entirely ceased and death followed but his mind would no longer function. A sickening feeling of revulsion mixed with pity overwhelmed him as the distressing feeling that started in his hands now gripped his entire body. Terrified with the feeling that his heart was about to stop beating as his pulse slowed to a rate that was incompatible with life, he thought he was going to pass out. Without an understanding of what was happening, he panicked and appeared to falter. Karen was alarmed by his bizarre reaction and as he placed Heinrich in bed, she pulled him aside to move him out of the room away from his patient. As Paul was leaving the bedside, the monk gently touched his hand holding it momentarily to kiss it. Tears welled up in the physician's eyes as he walked away in the corridor and he began to cry uncontrollably.

The Monsignor sat down next to him trying to calm down his consultant, but he was consumed by emotional turmoil. After a while, realizing how he had responded, Paul regained his composure and apologized for his embarrassing reaction. The priest told him there was no need to apologize, and Karen murmured the same response but couldn't fathom why he had cried. She had never seen a grown man cry so hysterically. The priest was sympathetic and didn't think Paul's reaction was abnormal or uncommon. He had seen men break down and cry similarly with the trauma of witnessing near-death experiences during battle.

Paul told them, "Heinrich is critical and near death. Treatment has to begin immediately, and he must be moved to a critical care unit in a hospital, and not remain in a monastery ill-equipped to care for him."

Father Muller answered, "He won't consent to hospitalization. I have tried many times to persuade him. Whatever we do has to begin here. Moving him to a strange environment will hasten his death."

Paul said, "I'm am sure I can't give him the care he needs under these conditions."

The priest asked, "What do you need to treat him?"

Paul said, "Heinrich needs continuous monitoring and treatment with intravenous fluids, vitamins, and nourishment."

Karen interrupted and asked, "Wouldn't a feeding tube in his stomach be adequate for nourishment?"

Paul explained he was too sick for that and it would kill him. All his internal organs were shutting down and he'd die by filling his stomach with liquids that he could vomit and without sufficient strength to cough, fill his lungs causing pneumonia. The kind of medical care the friar required could only be provided in a hospital, he insisted. Muller, however, refused to back down and repeatedly asked what was needed to treat him in the monastery. Thwarted, Paul gave him a list of supplies and drugs, adding that treatment had to start immediately or else Heinrich would be flying with the angels in heaven. The Monsignor said he'd call the local hospital and have someone pick up whatever was needed.

Karen's tolerance for the entire melodrama of Paul's hysteria, the oppressive monastery, a dying monk and a gun-wielding priest was more than she wished to endure and wanted to get the hell out of there. Unable to eliminate the vision of his crying from her mind she asked Paul what he was feeling at the time and what caused it. Unwilling to discuss it with her, he decided to give her a generic answer about treating patients who were near death. She knew that it wasn't the first patient he had treated in that state and thought he was hiding something from her. Not giving up, she pressed on more forcibly, and relenting he described his recurring nightmares, that he had never discussed with anyone. Karen remarked that his dreams were not that unusual and, everyone had experienced similar nightmares. The frequent recurring dreams, he believed predicted something terrible that would occur in the future, and now he understood them as foretelling the frightening incident that he experienced while examining Heinrich. Believing it was a powerful mysterious energy laboring within the monk that was Heinrich's soul struggling to escape from his body, it physically and emotionally overpowered Paul to stop him from caring for his patient.

He said, "It was the most terrifying thing I have ever endured."

With a solemn tone he continued, "Perhaps a higher power called me to come to Andorra to help Friar Heinrich survive."

She thought he'd gone mad and with biting sarcasm said, "God didn't call you to come to Andorra for the monk, I did!"

Her remark typified what Paul had known was an ice-cold personality, and he shrugged his shoulders expressing the hopelessness of trying to explain to her an experience as personal and spiritual as the one he had been through.

She continued in her unnerving business-like manner, and said, "I'm not sticking around to wait while you treat the monk so let's get the blood sample and mouth scraping for the DNA analysis before Heinrich drops dead."

He walked away feeling sorry for her.

After they obtained Heinrich's DNA, she informed the Monsignor that she had completed her work and was returning to the United States. Paul told him that he would stay to care for the sick monk until he showed improvement. Muller wasn't sure Heinrich would survive but told his consultant to remain at the monastery as long as was necessary.

She was so relieved to leave the uncomfortable monastic accommodations that she walked two miles to the road where they had parked the rental car and drove to Barcelona. There was surprising news waiting for her when she arrived. The FBI had gotten word that Doctor Reisbach was missing, and no one seemed to know where he was. The agency had booked her on a flight to New York on the following day but with further thought she concluded that he would escape to South America, and she decided to fly to Miami.

During the trip to Miami, she thought about her experience in Spain and Margarita, Heinrich's daughter who confirmed that Reisbach had lived in Buenos Aires and on a hunch, Karen had considered that if he escaped it would be to South

America. With a Canadian passport, it was easy to travel to Cuba and then to South America. Cuba, a short distance from the Florida Keys didn't require a commercial flight to get him there and was easily accessed by boat or private jet. While she eagerly awaited the plane to land in Miami and begin her chase, she hoped to stop him before he got that far and catch him in South Florida before he reached Cuba. She would leave the samples taken from the monk for the DNA analysis with the Miami FBI even though she had planned to hand carry it to Washington DC and personally deliver it to headquarters. Stopping Reisbach on the run was more important than her personal delivery of his brother's DNA.

Happy to leave Andorra and not have to listen to Paul's whining anymore, she felt vaguely contrite about deserting him there to manage on his own. Although she had become fond of him and his role that contributed to finding the twin brother, his strange behavior with foreign women and the strange reaction with Heinrich worried her. She wondered what would become of him and his fling with Angela. Karen thought the relationship wouldn't last and like those with most female hot tamales it eventually would cool down as she'd became a royal pain in the ass. Predicting Paul would eventually return to his wife, she concluded that he required a structured existence that only a gal like Maria could control. With an obligation confining him to the nest, her guess was it was all the freedom he could safely handle. With Maria's pressure Paul would finally relent and return to her. She laughed while reflecting on how her fellow agents would react after telling them about the last episode of Paul's hysterical reaction with the monk that she had witnessed. After planning to spend long days searching for Reisbach, exhausted, she fell asleep during the remaining time on the flight to Miami.

Paul had recovered from his unnerving experience with Heinrich and sent the monk's blood to the hospital for analysis while he waited for the long list of supplies and medications that were promised by the Monsignor. He explained to his new patient that he would require an intravenous tube in his arm to supply fluids, nutrients and blood tests for a while until he was strong enough to be fed. Having confidence in his physician, Heinrich accepted the treatment without resistance. Paul wished to get a chest x-ray and monitoring devices but bringing any equipment to the monastery or the friar's bedside was impossible. Aware that counting on information obtained from blood tests and clinical assessment alone would not effectively monitor the treatment, he had no other options. Unless the monk appeared to respond quickly, treatment would be a predictable failure causing his death from an inadequate attempt to treat his ravaged body.

While waiting for medical supplies, his thoughts turned to Angela. He didn't know how long he would need to stay in the monastery caring for the brother. Being the only person providing care for someone in a desperate state, he would not be able to leave for days and didn't want to jeopardize his relationship with her. An idea occurred to him that Angela might spend time in the monastery and assist him, however reflecting on it, he knew that would not happen. He was beginning to have misgivings about it when one of the monks interrupted his train of thought. Standing there with a large box containing IV tubing, needles, and intravenous fluids, the monk was waiting for Paul to start treating his patient.

Chapter Fifteen

Reisbach had asked the hospital for a medical leave and because of his years of service and advanced age it was granted immediately. There were many available surgeons trained by him who could cover during his absence. He was held in high esteem as a physician and educator as well as being a noted researcher. One of the top physicians in the country within his specialty, he had impeccable credentials and made significant contributions to medicine which accorded the privilege of sidestepping many rules and regulations that affected other physicians. His fame hadn't hindered the FBI surveillance of him that began after Karen and Paul departed for Puerto Rico. His vacation home and property in northern New York State near the Canadian border were staked out by FBI agents. Since he maintained dual citizenships in the United States and Canada, he had valid passports from both countries. The Canadian and Mexican authorities had been notified to detain him if he attempted to enter their nations with either passport and he had been placed on no-fly lists if he tried to leave the States. The FBI had sent a team of agents to the village nearest his country home in upstate New York to survey the town. They had interviewed all the merchants in town trying to uncover any business dealings with them and the townsfolk. They were unable to collect any useful information because no one knew who he was. Apparently, he never had business dealings with any of the local shops or dined at the restaurants in town. It was evident that his residence and identity were well-kept secrets from the community. The agency thought he would have employed some of the local citizens to take care of his everyday needs; however, no one in the town of a few thousand people knew of anyone in the village who had ever worked for him. If there were caretakers of his home and property, their existence was unknown. The FBI assumed that he hired people from outside the community and there were no records of purchases that were probably paid for in cash by the hired help. For him to continue to recruit aides who were not recognized in town required using different individuals from different areas that rotated at intervals long enough to make them anonymous. It was the perfect ploy in a small community that was frequented by visitors who traveled there on vacation or merely as a pitstop while driving to Canada since it was a short distance from the border.

His home was separated by acres of land from all the major roadways, and the neighbors seldom saw him and didn't know who he was. It was a perfect place for someone to hide or escape to Canada. To maintain that degree of secrecy, the FBI realized that he had constructed a system that granted him the ability to live in complete anonymity from the intrusion of the outside world. They also realized that employing caretakers for his affairs and property who were unknown to the local population required the use of some other source than the community. The outside source would require a significant number of people who could be relied upon to maintain secrecy which excluded employment agencies. The only organization that could help a former Nazi in that way would have been one of the larger Neo-Nazi groups in the country. Karen was familiar with those in the Northwest and was certain there were affiliates in rural New York that she did not know about. It was apparent that an exceptionally devious mind with the aid of an underground organization had devised a plan to remain undetected long before the FBI operation began.

With the information she had received from the FBI investigating his country residence, Karen determined that escaping the country from his country home was a too risky a ploy for him to use and she changed her flight to Miami. The two factors influencing her decision included the United States not having an extradition treaty with Cuba, and Havana's location ninety miles from Key West, Florida. He could remain in Cuba indefinitely without worrying about capture or being returned to the States by the authorities in Havana. Reports in FBI records indicated fifty to seventy fugitives from the USA lived there freely without fear of ever being apprehended to face justice in the United States. Karen didn't think Reisbach would make Cuba his home since he was too big a fish to settle in that small pond, and there was nothing on the small island he could exploit to his benefit. His destination had to be somewhere in South America where there were plenty of resources and opportunities available to network with young, and old Nazi types who would welcome him. Although the number of Nazis had dwindled since the time he had lived there as a medical student, there were dictatorships continuing to function on the continent offering a platform for all kinds of fascist activity. With his knowledge of the customs and language, it was the perfect choice for an old war criminal to spend the remaining years of his life.

The Florida Keys served as the logical place from which he could escape to Cuba. She had notified the Miami agency to start the search for him in Miami and expanded it south to Homestead and Florida City. Located in the southern most region of the Florida mainland, they were gateways to the Everglades and Keys which were known as secure places for fugitives and the drug trade to hide. The Everglades with its dense jungle and abundant alligator population helped criminals to avoid capture. The many islands and diverse water formations there and in the Keys were well-known for frustrating law enforcement efforts to search, find and trap criminals. The Keys positioned below the southern tip of the Florida mainland are connected to Florida City, the last stop on the east coast, by the Overseas Highway ending one hundred and twenty-eight miles in the southern most city in the United States, Key West.

The highway travels south over land and water comprised of multiple islands surrounded by thousands of different bodies of water that vary from bays to lagoons. The unique chain of islands separating the Atlantic Ocean from the Gulf of Mexico are known as the Florida Keys in Monroe County Florida. The variety of places to hide on land or water compound the difficulty created by the tropical land masses and surrounding saltwater where there are many places to hole up in from posh resorts to trailer parks and sleazy motels. Plenty of condominiums, homes or yachts are available to take cover in and rent by the day, week or month. An individual could find many secluded beaches to hide for a while if their body could tolerate the heat and mosquitos.

Karen with a small corps of FBI agents combing all the localities and sites were hoping for some lead on him. The Coast Guard was on alert checking marinas and keeping a watch for boats traveling into Cuban waters. If he made it to Key West, it was a short trip to Havana. After the mainland, the first key to explore was Key Largo which spans twenty-seven miles in length and three miles at its widest section. It's known for boating, fishing and some beautiful places to soak up the sun's rays. On the northeastern tip of the island, there was an exclusive private club enjoyed only by the wealthiest one percent of the population in the country, and during the summer, many affluent Miamians enjoyed themselves there. The property located on the Atlantic Ocean twenty miles from downtown Key Largo was known as the Atlantic Reef Club. It was the perfect place for privacy and required a membership to belong or own property there, however a guest could stay there with a member's referral.

In the summer, the scene was less crowded, with more visitors occupying the resort on the weekend than during the remainder of the week. With a hotel, several restaurants, a small village with shopping, cultural center, private airport, and hotel, it had every amenity that wealth could afford.

The claim was that the property was listed by the FBI as the safest place to live on the east coast of America and it was a gated, well-guarded private community that boasted three golf courses, tennis and croquet courses and one of the largest private marinas in the country. The average citizen could never hope to belong to it or live there unless they had won a giant lottery jackpot. Karen and her team made a surprise visit so as not to alert anyone staying there. No one in resort's security or management offices had been notified of their visit, and she drove up to the entrance gate showing her credentials, asking to see the head of security.

The club's staff was very cooperative, and the FBI agents devoted several hours to scouring lists of seasonal and permanent residents including the recently invited guests. The number of guests and residents had decreased during the summer months since the majority were snow-birds who had taken off to their elegant residences in the north. The security officer found that an elderly man who was a recent guest referred by a New York member had arrived three days earlier and departed the morning the agents arrived. He hadn't registered using Reisbach's name, however it was assumed an alias was used. She was confident from the description provided by the security officer that it was the surgeon. Disappointed that she had missed the visitor, she was relieved that they weren't that far behind him. The remainder of Key Largo was covered the same day with no positive leads, and they ended the day in Islamorada, known for its Tarpon and Marlin fishing. That's where the big blue water fish of the Atlantic Ocean were caught by the big boys in their big boats and for Karen it turned out to be a day without catching Reisbach.

By the end of the third day, Karen received news from the Monroe County police department that a man fitting his description was seen in a private community in the city of Marathon located in the middle of the Keys forty-eight miles from Key West. It was an excellent location for someone attempting to escape to Cuba from the small airport in town where a private plane could take off relatively unnoticed or a small power boat rented from any of the many marinas could make it to Havana within the day. They checked the local airport and marinas for departure documents listing a senior citizen fitting the fugitive's description. At the airport, they learned that an elderly gentleman had inquired about flying to Cuba on the preceding day. Although the airport had been listed as an international airport, he was told no international flights were leaving from there.

Marathon was one of the busiest locations during the winter months because it is a commercial center approximately equidistant between the beginning and end of the Keys. It contained the only Home Depot after leaving Florida City and before reaching Key West. During the summer, the agents didn't have to deal with the crowds of shopping visitors and workmen of the winter months that would have made scouting the region more difficult. Karen knew they were fifty miles from their destination and she was headed to Key West, hot on Reisbach's trail. An hour away and south of Marathon, she left behind some of her crew to search the smaller properties of Little Palm Island and Hawks Cay that were on the way. Little Palm Island, the small tropical paradise three miles off the Atlantic shore of Big Pine Key was only accessible by boat or seaplane and offered lots of tropical vegetation and tall palm trees with small pristine cottages on five acres of land surrounded by water. Karen could only hope for another opportunity to see the exotic island since she left some of her crew behind to assess it while she went to Key West. A handful of agents followed her to the Conch Republic as the city of Key West was called. The town at one time had aspired to secede as the Conch Republic a small nation located off the North American continent. Enlisting the harbor patrol for help, they boarded every sailboat and yacht that was moored or docked in the marinas on the island, looking for him. Accompanied by two agents, she and her men surveyed the records of every hotel, motel and guest house on the main thoroughfare, Duval Street and its adjacent side streets in town. Towards the end of the day, she sent them to investigate the other side of the island that included the the international airport.

Summer days were steaming hot and humid in the sunlight until late in the day and working in the sweltering heat drained their energy. Despite being out of season, the harbor and Duval Street where the vacationers gathered, were as crowded as during the peak tourist months. Cruise ships were docked in port, and the place was bustling with visitors who weren't bothered by the scorching heat. Late in the day, Karen stopped to have dinner at an outdoor cafe on the main thoroughfare. She decided to find a restaurant on

Duval Street to study the passing crowds. Finding one with an elevated patio facing the sidewalk along the street, there was a table that enabled her to see clearly down to the harbor over the heads of passersby. After eating she had planned to walk to the harbor's promenade and afterward return to the motel at sunset to confer with her agents. As she waited for her dinner to be served, she saw an elderly man two blocks away walking towards her on Duval who abruptly turned on Greene Street. It was Reisbach, and she quickly got up and ran down to the sidewalk and the street he had turned on. Pushing her way through the crowds, she arrived at the corner and looking down the block saw him heading towards Front Street on the harbor. Running to catch up, she lost sight of him and stopped at the docks in the port. The boat slips were close to where large crowds had gathered to be entertained by jugglers and other street performers. She stopped to glance at the people circling the performers and didn't see him. The sun appearing like a giant orange balloon lowering on the horizon cast its vibrant red hue on the water and blinded her as she approached the end of the wharf. Averting her gaze from the sun's reflection, while turning her head to look elsewhere, she saw a small island across from the body of water that separated the island from the promenade. Although the harbor patrol had explored the harbor during the day, in her mind, there was a good chance that his sudden disappearance from sight during her chase meant he had fled to the island. There were homes there, and commandeering a small boat, he could have quickly headed there. The sun had not set into the horizon, and she had to find a way to get across to the island and find him while there still was some daylight. Running back to the harbor, she found a patrol boat nearby with two officers waiting until darkness when most of the crowds dispersed. Showing her credentials, she asked them to take her to the small island to look for a fugitive. They told her they couldn't leave until there was no one remaining on the promenade. She claimed it was a matter of national security requiring the capture of a dangerous criminal alien fleeing the country. It wasn't entirely the truth, but it seemed to work. They called for emergency backup and began heading towards the island. She asked about the homes located there and was told that they were privately owned and mainly occupied during the winter months. Questioning them if any were recently moved into, they told her that one had been rented in the past week. The officers had a list of current occupants since they regularly patrolled the area looking for vandals and burglars. She asked them to take her slowly by boat around the isle to find the home that was recently occupied. While close to shore, she borrowed a pair of binoculars from one of the men and tried to see into the interior of the homes at the water's edge. Through the window of one of the houses, she thought she saw a television screen that was on. She asked the officer to check his list to see if it was the home that was recently rented. He confirmed it was the one and they beached the boat within walking distance from the house. As they walked towards the home, she asked the officers to remain outside. The front door was unlocked, and she walked into a dark hallway. Walking in the hall voices were heard that appeared to come from the television. Believing it was originating from the rear of the house that faced the water, she quietly walked into the room, and saw the top of a man's head who was sitting in a high back lounge chair watching television. Nervously not certain it was him, she called out his name, Doctor Reisbach. He arose from the chair and turned to face her. Blocked by the chair, all she saw was his face and the upper half of his torso. The lower half of his body, including the forearms, and hands, were hidden from view by the chair.

Reisbach casually said, "I thought that was you I saw on Duval."

Still unsettled by unexpectedly finding him, she told him in a commanding voice, "You are under arrest for the murders of the individuals in New York and Idaho and the war crimes you committed during the World War Two."

She had sensed that finding him like that was too easy and suspicious that something wasn't right, thought it was a trap. A bit jittery about not being able to see his hands hidden in the dark room, she asked Reisbach to step away from the chair, but he didn't budge.

He calmly asked her, "What proof do you have that I am guilty of all those crimes you have accused me of?"

She told him, "Your surgical assistant and assassin was killed attempting to murder my deputy and me. We have DNA evidence that proves that you are not the twin who you claim to be. Furthermore, it shows that you are the mass murderer who assisted Doctor Mengele in the concentration camp at Auschwitz."

"What makes you think that I am the murderer and not my brother who hides behind an angelic pretense of silence and prayer in a monastery?" he replied.

She answered, "You'll see the evidence in court," and she moved towards him to handcuff him.

He moved away behind the chair and told her, "You're just as bold and unafraid as your father."

She had no idea what he was talking about as she moved closer to place the handcuffs on his wrists.

Taunting her more he said, "You even look like your father."

Maddened by his remarks, she asked, "What difference does it make if I resemble my dad, who you murdered and was so unlike you?"

With a sarcastic smirk on his face, he told her, "That man wasn't your real father, he was a substitute."

Bewildered she didn't know where the conversation was leading and moved back staring at him. Confused, she didn't know what he was trying to tell her.

She continued, "I know he worked for you, and you had him murdered."

He answered in an arrogant tone of voice, "That man wasn't your real father."

"What are you saying?" she shouted!

Continuing he said, "You really don't know who your real father is, do you?"

"Compare your DNA to mine, and you will find out who he is."

She looked at him more closely and saw an old man with facial features that resembled many German men his age.

Suddenly she stopped and hesitated a few seconds. With fury in her voice, she said, "Are you telling me, you're my father? My dad was a gentleman who was warm and loving unlike you or my mother."

Not stopping, he persisted, "That man was a surrogate for me. Your mother and I were lovers, and she was pregnant with you, our child! I could not continue my life's work with a wife and a child."

Karen responding in a rage said, "Because you impregnated my mother, doesn't make you my father. You were the surrogate and nothing more than a sperm donor. Fathers give their children love and don't abandon them. You're a disgrace and will die disgraced!" as she walked forward to cuff him.

While stepping towards him, she was having difficulty seeing his movement in the increasingly darkened room. She thought he had moved closer to the chair and began to raise his arm hidden by the chair as though reaching for a handgun.

She quickly drew her gun and before he could lift his arm further, shot him. He fell to the floor, and she ran to him to see if he was dead. He was lying on the floor alert and grasping his arm that was bleeding. He said it wasn't necessary to shoot him. As he was passing out, she heard him say that he deserved it but couldn't have shot her without a gun. She realized she had fired at a man who was unarmed and claimed to be her biological father. The harbor patrolmen heard the gunfire and ran into the house with their weapons drawn. They saw her tying a makeshift tourniquet around his upper arm and asked them to look for something to carry him out to the boat with. They grabbed an oriental rug that had been in the hallway and with it brought him to the patrol boat. Rushing to the harbor with the boat siren blasting, they transported him to an ambulance that had remained stationed at the promenade. His vital signs were stable, as they rushed him to the hospital.

Karen was wholly unnerved about mistakenly shooting the surgeon who didn't have a gun and was possibly her father. She became teary eyed and on the verge of crying while waiting at the hospital for the report of Reisbach's condition from the emergency room physician. They had completed his physical exam and preliminary blood tests and determined that there wasn't a significant amount of blood loss and he was stable. The bullet had grazed his upper arm just below the shoulder, and he would recover. The doctors decided to keep him overnight in the hospital because of his age and since he was under arrest. She stationed agents outside his hospital room and left for the motel. At the motel, she broke down and cried continuously before falling asleep on the bed.

Epilogue

Karen became despondent following the realization that the man she had sought for years to bring to justice for war crimes and murder was her biological father. She had pursued him aggressively in large part because of her love for her adopted father but now the inner turmoil created by her dominant role in his arrest was an emotional crisis that confused her and she fought desperately to overcome. Accepting the fact that her existence was the product of the sexual union between a cold-blooded psychopathic serial killer and a cold, detached unloving mother was what troubled her the most. Reflecting on her life, she ruminated incessantly about how her genetic birthright influenced her behavior. Although the history of her paternal parentage revealed a physically abusive grandfather with a murdering son, she couldn't fathom the reason for her mother's lack of affection for her only daughter. She pondered over her life experiences and agonized about how life would have been if the circumstances surrounding her childhood and early adult life had been different. Many questions arose in her mind about her aggressiveness in life and her career. Her relationships with others and the choices she had made in the past led her to believe that her fundamental inability to trust anyone and suspicions about forming close and lifelong relationships were the consequences of her heredity. Like an animal licking their wounds, the repetitive negative thoughts kept requiring intercessions based on temporary self-help that was driving her to the point of mental exhaustion.

She received praise at work for her determination and professionalism in concluding a lengthy criminal investigation that ended with the capture of her real father. While awaiting Reisbach's trial for war crimes and murder, she was promoted to a higher rank at the FBI and offered a chance to head her own division on international crime. She hadn't decided to take the offer and didn't want to return to her former agency in Idaho. The awards and accolades she received from the FBI did nothing to heal the chronic wounds inflicted by the self-doubt of how things in her life were conditioned by inherited traits. She was promoted to assistant bureau chief for her admirable work and given a leave of absence to work out her problems and receive counseling for the emotional trauma sustained from the rigors of her accomplishment. Even though the FBI had many ways to help their agents who experienced difficulty with similar types of psychological crises, she believed that accepting their help would reveal a weakness in her that was not approved of in the male-dominated world of the FBI. She had very few options available to seek outside help and had no family or friends to fall back on. This bothered her terribly and motivated her to consider individual professional advice. There was an awareness however that uncovering her true self might be devastating and it prevented her from seeking psychiatric treatment.

She required a compassionate individual to guide her, and the only person she knew like that was Paul Peres. She mulled over how to approach the topic with him and hesitated to call him. Fortunately, she was aware that he had tried to contact her several times to congratulate her on the successful capture of Reisbach and the many awards that she had received. Badly in need of someone, she could confide in and discuss her emotional discord, she picked up the phone and called him. The premise she used was to find out how he was progressing with his treatment of the monk. She knew the brother had survived his severe malnutrition with Paul's dedicated care. Although he was recovering, the possibility that he would recover full function remained questionable in her mind.

Paul was happy to hear from her and praised her for the awards and promotion she had received from the FBI. He had also heard that the Israeli government was honoring her with a medal for the determination and perseverance she exhibited in tracking down Doctor Reisbach, the Angel of Death's assistant. It was upsetting to learn that the surgeon turned out to be her biological father, and she had shot and wounded him. With all the time he had to think about it, he assumed that she had to be pretty messed up psychologically because of all her efforts to solve crimes in which her father was the perpetrator of all the horrific deeds that she attributed to someone else. If it were Paul or anyone else, it would have wholly unhinged them. He desperately wanted to know how she was holding up but had not called to ask her directly. After the usual small talk, she asked him how he was dealing with the divorce and when it would be finalized.

The divorce had been finalized, and the papers were signed. Karen didn't reveal that she knew all the details and had influenced the lawyers to come to a mutual agreement. That led her to ask about Angela and his relationship with her. Without hesitation, he told her they were considering marriage. She was surprised that it was even a consideration before the ink on the divorce papers had dried but happy to hear that, she wished them well. Expressing how glad he was, he replied that all the conflict that was experienced in the past had magically disappeared and he no longer was having the nightmares or the doubts about his career. He wanted her to know that in a short while he would be returning home with his new wife, Angela. That remark almost floored her, but she answered that she looked forward to seeing them. He added that they were planning to be married by the monsignor in a quiet ceremony in the monastery before leaving Andorra. She didn't know how to respond and said it sounded beautiful. In a reflective tone, he asked how she was getting along. Admitting that her entire career had been motivated by the need to capture a villain that culminated with the shocking realization that it was her father, she wasn't doing well emotionally. Being sympathetic, he responded it was understandable and related that he had terrible conflicts about his past decisions that had required professional help. He wasn't surprised by her admission that she had considered consulting someone to help her with her problem and was in a jam on how to proceed since she feared repercussions at work. He said he knew all about that, and it wasn't easy for him as a doctor to take that step. Psychiatric help for physicians was not well received by their peers and patients and said he had to go about it in complete secrecy. Hearing and feeling his empathy was a great relief to her and she asked him if he had any ideas about who she should see. He told her that he didn't know anyone in Idaho but would look into finding someone there he could refer her to. She told him that she would be staying in New York for a while with occasional trips to Washington D.C until the trial of her father had concluded. In that case, he said he would be happy to refer her to the psychiatrist that he had consulted and would call him to explain her situation and set up an appointment. Affirming that he would arrange for the visit with the doctor on a date when she planned to be in New York, he mentioned that he would be returning to the city in a few weeks with Angela after they received the documents for her to enter the country. Wanting to see him and Angela again, she suggested they could go to the Mexican restaurant in Spanish Harlem for dinner. He laughed and said it was a deal.

Paul was anxious to get home with his new love Angela after caring for the friar who had fully recovered. In Westchester, he had become a celebrity and had been written up in the local newspapers. With his new reputation, an offer to author a book on his international crime-fighting exploits was being considered. Although he had had doubts that he still held a job when he returned to New York, the FBI had secured his position as promised. He would return as the

Director of the Medical Clinic and be made Chief of Internal Medicine and given an appointment at the university. Doctors Stark and Stern were fired because they had conspired with Reisbach to falsify the results of the anti-rejection drug that had been reported to the FDA. They were being investigated by the federal government for their complicity in promoting a drug despite its adverse effects. The research program to cure diabetes continued under the direction of a new head of the department appointed by the university. The entire administration of the hospital and its board were replaced by people assigned by the medical school after the final take-over of the hospital.

Printed in the United States
By Bookmasters